Valentino and *Sagittarius*

Also by Natalia Ginzburg
and available in Seaver Books

All Our Yesterdays
Family Sayings
The Little Virtues
The City and the House
The Manzoni Family

Natalia Ginzburg

TWO NOVELLAS

VALENTINO

AND

SAGITTARIUS

Translated from the Italian
by Avril Bardoni

Seaver Books
Henry Holt and Company
New York

First published in the United States in 1988 by
Seaver Books / Henry Holt and Company, Inc.,
115 West 18th Street,
New York, New York 10011.
Valentino and *Sagittarius* were originally published in
Italy under the title *Cinque romanzi brevi*.

Library of Congress Cataloging-in-Publication Data
Ginzburg, Natalia.
Valentino ; and, Sagittarius.
Translation: Valentino and Sagittario.
I. Ginzburg, Natalia. Sagittario. English. 1988.
II. Title.   III. Title: Valentino.   IV. Title:
Sagittarius.
PQ4817.I5V313   1988   853′.912   87-32349
ISBN: 0-8050-0683-4

First American Edition

Printed in the United States of America
1 3 5 7 9 10 8 6 4 2

ISBN 0-8050-0683-4

CONTENTS

VALENTINO

I LIVED with my father, mother and brother in a small rented apartment in the middle of town. Life was not easy and finding the rent money was always a problem. My father was a retired school-teacher and my mother gave piano lessons; we had to help my sister who was married to a commercial traveller and had three children and a pitifully inadequate income, and we also had to support my student brother who my father believed was destined to become a man of consequence. I attended a teacher-training college and in my spare time helped the caretaker's children with their homework. The caretaker had relatives who lived in the country and she paid in kind with a supply of chestnuts, apples and potatoes.

My brother was studying medicine and the expenses were never-ending: microscope, books, fees . . . My father believed that he was destined to become a man of consequence. There was little enough reason to believe this, but he believed it all the same and had done ever since Valentino was a small boy and perhaps found it difficult to break the habit. My father spent his days in the kitchen, dreaming and muttering to himself, fantasizing about the future when Valentino would be a famous doctor and attend medical congresses in the great capitals and discover new drugs and new diseases. Valentino himself seemed devoid of any ambition to become a man of consequence; in the house, he usually spent his time playing with a kitten or making toys for the caretaker's children out of scraps of old material stuffed with sawdust, fashioning cats and dogs and monsters too, with big heads and long, lumpy bodies. Or he would don his skiing outfit and admire himself in the mirror; not that he went skiing very often, for he was lazy and hated the cold, but he had persuaded my mother to make him an outfit all in black with a great white woollen balaclava; he thought himself no end of a fine fellow in these clothes and would strut about in front of the mirror first with a scarf thrown about his neck and then without and would go out on to the balcony so that the caretaker's children could see him.

Many times he had become engaged and then broken it off and my mother had had to clean the dining-room specially and dress for the occasion. It had happened so often already that when he announced that he was getting married within the month nobody believed him, and my mother cleaned the dining-room wearily and put on the grey silk dress reserved for her pupils' examinations at the Conservatory and for meeting Valentino's prospective brides.

We were expecting a girl like all the others he had promised to marry and then dropped after a couple of weeks, and by this time we thought we knew the type that appealed to him: teenagers wearing jaunty little berets and still studying at high-school. They were usually very shy and we never felt threatened by them, partly because we knew he would drop them and partly because they looked just like my mother's piano pupils.

So when he turned up with his new fiancée we were amazed to the point of speechlessness. She was quite unlike anything we had ever imagined. She was wearing a longish sable coat and flat rubber-soled shoes and was short and fat. From behind tortoise-shell glasses she regarded us with hard, round eyes. Her nose was shiny and she had a moustache. On her head she wore a black hat squashed down on one side and the hair not covered by the hat was black streaked with grey, crimped and untidy. She was at least ten years older than Valentino.

Valentino talked non-stop because we were incapable of speech. He talked about a hundred things all at once, about the cat and the caretaker's children and his microscope. He wanted to take his fiancée to his room at once to show her the microscope but my mother objected because the room had not been tidied. And his fiancée said that she had seen plenty of microscopes anyway. So Valentino went to find the cat and brought it to her. He had tied a ribbon with a bell around its neck to make it look pretty, but the cat was so frightened by the bell that it raced up the curtain and clung there, hissing and glaring at us, its fur all on end and its eyes gleaming ferociously and my mother began to moan with apprehension lest her curtain should be ruined.

Valentino's fiancée lit a cigarette and began to talk. The tone of her voice was that of a person used to giving orders and everything she said was like a command. She told us that she loved Valentino and had every confidence in him; she was confident that he would give up playing with the cat and making toys. And she said that she had a great deal of money so they could marry without having to wait for Valentino to start earning. She was alone and had no ties since both her parents were dead and she was answerable to no one.

All at once my mother started to cry. It was an awkward moment and nobody knew quite what to do. There was absolutely no emotion behind my mother's tears except grief and shock; I sensed this and felt sure that the others sensed it too. My father patted her knee and made little clicking noises with his tongue as if comforting a child. Valentino's fiancée suddenly became very red in the face and she went over to my mother; her eyes gleamed, alarmed and imperious at the same time, and I realized that she intended to marry Valentino come what may. 'Oh dear, Mother's crying,' said Valentino, 'but Mother does tend to get emotional.' — 'Yes,' said my mother, and she dried her eyes, patted her hair and drew herself up. 'I'm not very strong at the moment and tears come easily. This news has taken me rather by surprise; but Valentino has always done whatever he wanted to do.' My mother had had a genteel education; her behaviour was always correct and she had great self-control.

Valentino's fiancée told us that she and Valentino were

11

going to buy furniture for the sitting-room that very day. Nothing else needed to be bought as her house already contained all that they would need. And Valentino sketched a plan, for my mother's benefit, of the house in which his fiancée had lived since her childhood and in which they would now live together: it had three floors and a garden and was in a neighbourhood where all the houses were detached and each had its own garden.

For a little while after they had gone we all sat silently looking at each other. Then my mother told me to go and fetch my sister, and I went.

My sister lived in a top-floor flat on the outskirts of town. All day long she typed addresses for a firm that paid her so much for each addressed envelope. She had constant toothache and kept a scarf wrapped round her face. I told her that our mother wanted to see her and she asked why but I wouldn't tell her. Intensely curious, she picked up the youngest child and came with me.

My sister had never believed that Valentino was destined to become a man of consequence. She couldn't stand him and pulled a face every time his name was mentioned, remembering all the money my father spent on his education while she was forced to type addresses. Because of this, my mother had never told her about the skiing outfit and whenever my sister came to our house one of us had to rush to his room and make sure that these clothes and any other new things that he had bought for himself were out of sight.

It was not easy to explain to my sister Clara the turn that events had taken. That a woman had appeared with lashings of money and a moustache who was willing to pay for the privilege of marrying Valentino and that he had agreed; that he had left all the teenagers in berets behind him and was now shopping in town for sitting-room furniture with a woman who wore a sable coat. His drawers were still full of photographs of the teenage girls and the letters they had written him. And after his marriage to the bespectacled and moustachioed woman he would still manage somehow to slip away from time to time to meet the teenagers in berets and would spend a little money on their amusements; only a little, because he was basically mean when it came to spending on others the money he regarded as his own.

Clara sat and listened to my father and mother and shrugged her shoulders. Her toothache was very bad and addresses were waiting to be typed; she also had the washing to do and her children's socks to mend. Why had we dragged her out and made her come all this way and forced her to waste a whole afternoon? She wasn't the slightest bit interested in Valentino, in what he did or whom he married; the woman was doubtless mad because only a mad woman could seriously want to marry Valentino; or she was a whore who had found her dupe and the fur coat was probably fake — Father and Mother had no idea about furs. My mother insisted that the fur was genuine, that the woman was certainly respectable and that her manners and bearing were those of a lady, and she was not mad; only ugly, as ugly as sin. And at the memory of that ugliness my mother covered her face with her hands and started to cry again. But my father said that that was not the main consideration; and he was about to launch into a long speech about what was the main consideration but my mother interrupted him. My mother always interrupted his speeches, leaving him choking on a half-finished sentence, puffing with frustration.

There was a sudden clamour in the hall: Valentino was back. He had found Clara's little boy there and was greeting him boisterously, swinging him high over his head and then down to the floor, then up and down again while the baby screamed with laughter. For a moment Clara seemed to enjoy the laughter of her child, but her face soon darkened with the emotions of spite and bitterness that the sight of Valentino invariably aroused in her.

Valentino started to describe the furniture they had bought for the sitting-room. It was Empire style. He told us how much it had cost, quoting sums that to us seemed enormous; he rubbed his hands together hard and tossed the figures gleefully around our little living-room. He took out a cigarette and lit it; he had a gold lighter — a present from Maddalena, his fiancée.

He was oblivious of the uneasy silence which gripped the rest of us. My mother avoided looking at him. My sister had picked up her little boy and was pulling on his gloves. Since the appearance of the gold cigarette lighter, her lips had been compressed into a grim smile which she now concealed behind her scarf as she left, carrying her child. As she passed through the door, the word 'Pig!' filtered through the scarf.

The word had been uttered very softly, but Valentino heard it. He started after Clara, intending to follow her downstairs and ask her why she had called him a pig and my mother held him back with difficulty. 'Why did she say that?' Valentino asked my mother. 'Why did the wretched woman call me a pig? Because I'm getting married? Is that why I'm a pig? What's she thinking about, the old hag!'

My mother smoothed the pleats in her dress, sighed and said nothing; my father refilled his pipe with fingers that trembled. He struck a match against the sole of his shoe to light his pipe but Valentino, noticing this, went up to him holding out his cigarette lighter. My father glanced at Valentino's hand proffering the light, then he suddenly pushed the hand away, threw down his pipe and left the room. A moment later he reappeared in the doorway, puffing and gesticulating as if about to launch into a speech; but then he thought better of it and turned away without a word, slamming the door behind him.

Valentino stood as if transfixed. 'But why?' he asked my mother. 'Why is he angry? What's the matter with them? What have I done wrong?'

'That woman is as ugly as sin,' said my mother quietly. 'She's grotesque, Valentino. And since she boasts about being so wealthy, everyone will assume that you are marrying her for her money. That's what we think too, Valentino, because we cannot believe that you are in love with her, you who always used to chase the pretty girls, none of whom was ever pretty enough for you. Nothing like this has ever happened in our family before; not one of us has ever done anything just for money.'

Valentino said we hadn't understood anything at all. His fiancée wasn't ugly, at least he didn't find her ugly, and wasn't his opinion the only one that really mattered? She had lovely black eyes and the bearing of a lady, apart from which she was intelligent, extremely intelligent and very cultured. He was bored with all those pretty little girls with nothing to talk about, while with Maddalena he could talk about books and a hundred other things. He wasn't marrying her for her money; he was no pig. Deeply offended all of a sudden, he went and shut himself in his room.

In the days that followed he continued to sulk and to act the part of a man marrying in the teeth of family opposition. He was solemn, dignified, rather pale and spoke to none of us. He never showed us the presents that he received from his fiancée but every day he had something new: on his wrist he sported a gold watch with a second hand and a white leather strap, he carried a crocodile-skin wallet and had a new tie every day.

My father said he would go to have a talk with Valentino's fiancée, but my mother was opposed to this, partly because my father had a weak heart and was supposed to avoid any excitement, partly because she thought his arguments would be completely ineffectual. My father never said anything sensible; perhaps what he meant to say was sensible enough, but he never managed to express what he meant, getting bogged down in empty words, digressions and childhood memories, stumbling and gesticulating. So at home he was never allowed to finish what he was saying because we were always too impatient, and he would hark back wistfully to his teaching days when he could talk as much as he wanted and nobody humiliated him.

My father had always been very diffident in his dealings with Valentino; he had never dared to reprove him even when he failed his examinations, and he had never ceased to believe that he would one day become a man of consequence. Now, however, this belief had apparently deserted him; he looked unhappy and seemed to have aged overnight. He no longer liked to stay alone in the kitchen, saying that it was airless and made him feel claustrophobic and he took to sitting outside the bar downstairs sipping vermouth; or sometimes he walked down to the river to watch the anglers, and returned puffing and muttering to himself.

So, seeing that it was the only thing that would set his mind at rest, my mother agreed to his going to see Valentino's fiancée. My father put on his best clothes and his best hat, too, and his gloves; and my mother and I stood on the balcony watching him go. And as we did so, a faint hope stirred within us that things would be sorted out for the best; we didn't know how this would come about nor even what we were hoping for precisely, and we certainly couldn't imagine what my father would find to say, but that afternoon was the most peaceful we had known for a long time. My father returned late looking very tired; he wanted to go straight to bed and my mother helped him to undress, questioning him while she did so; but this time it was he who was reluctant to talk. When he was in bed, with his eyes closed and his face ashen, he said: 'She's a good woman. I feel sorry for her.' And after a pause: 'I saw the house. A beautiful house, extremely elegant. The kind of elegance that is simply beyond the experience of people like you and me.' He was silent for a minute, then: 'Anyway, I'll soon be dead and buried.'

The wedding took place at the end of the month. My father wrote to one of his brothers asking for a loan, because we had to be well turned out so that we should not disgrace Valentino. For the first time in many years, my mother had a hat made for her: a tall, complicated creation with a bow and a little veiling. And she unearthed her old fox fur that had one eye missing; by arranging the tail carefully over the head she could hide this defect, and the hat had been so expensive that my mother was determined not to spend any more on this wedding. I had a new dress of pale blue wool trimmed with velvet, and around my neck I too had a little fox-fur, a tiny one that my aunt Giuseppina had given me for my ninth birthday. The most expensive item of all was the suit for Valentino, navy blue with a chalk stripe. He and my mother had gone together to choose it, and he had stopped sulking and was happy and said he had dreamed all his life of possessing a navy blue suit with a chalk stripe.

Clara announced that she had no intention of coming to the wedding because she wanted nothing to do with Valentino's disgraceful goings-on and had no money to waste; and Valentino told me to tell her to stay at home by all means as he would be happier if she spared him the sight of her ugly face on his wedding day. And Clara retorted that the bride's face was uglier than hers; she had only seen it in photographs but that was enough. But Clara did turn up in church after all, with her husband and eldest daughter; and they had taken pains to dress nicely and my sister had had her hair curled.

During the whole of the ceremony my mother held my hand and clutched it ever more tightly. During the exchange of rings she bent towards me and whispered that she couldn't bear to watch. The bride was in black and had on the same fur coat that she always wore and our caretaker who had been keen to come was disappointed because she had expected a veil and orange-blossom. She told us later that the wedding wasn't nearly as splendid as she had hoped after hearing all the rumours about Valentino marrying such a rich woman. Apart from the caretaker and the woman from the paper-shop on the corner, there was no one there that we knew; the church was full of Maddalena's acquaintances, well-dressed women in furs and jewels.

Afterwards we went to the house and were served with refreshments. Without even the caretaker and the woman from the paper-shop there, we felt utterly lost, my parents and I and Clara and Clara's husband. We huddled in a group close to the wall and Valentino came over to us for a moment to tell us not to stick together in a group like that; but we still stuck together. The garden and the ground-floor rooms of the house were crowded with all the people who had been in church; and Valentino moved easily among these people, speaking and being spoken to; he was very happy with his navy blue suit with a chalk stripe and took the ladies by the arm and led them to the buffet. The house was extremely elegant, as my father had said, and it was difficult to imagine that this was now Valentino's home.

Then the guests left and Valentino and his wife drove off in the car; they were to spend a three months honeymoon on the Riviera. We went home. Very excited by all the food she had eaten from the buffet and all the strange new things that she had seen, Clara's little girl jumped and skipped, chattering non-stop about how she had run round the garden and been frightened by a dog and how she had then gone into the kitchen and seen a tall cook all dressed in light blue, grinding coffee. But as soon as we were indoors our first thought was of the money that we owed to my father's brother. We were all tired and cross and my mother went to Valentino's room and sat on the unmade bed and had a little cry. But she soon started to tidy up the room and then put the mattress in mothballs, covered the furniture with dust-sheets and closed the shutters.

There seemed to be nothing to do now that Valentino had gone: no more clothes to brush or iron or spot with spirit. We seldom spoke about him for I was preparing for my exams and my mother spent much of her time with Clara, one of whose children was poorly. And my father took to wandering about the town because the solitary kitchen had become distasteful to him now; he sought out some of his old colleagues and attempted to indulge his taste for long speeches with them, but always ended up by saying that he might as well not bother as he would soon be dead anyway and he didn't mind dying since life had had precious little to offer. Occasionally the caretaker would come up to our flat bringing a little fruit in return for my help with her children's homework, and she invariably asked after Valentino and said how lucky we were that Valentino had married such a rich woman because she would set him up in a practice as soon as he qualified and we could sleep easy now that he was provided for; and if his wife was no beauty so much the better because at least one could be reasonably certain that she would never be unfaithful.

Summer drew to a close and Valentino wrote to say that they would not be back for a while yet; they were swimming and sailing and had planned a trip to the Dolomites. They were having a good holiday and wanted to enjoy it for as long as possible because once they returned to town they would have to work really hard. He had to prepare for his exams and his wife always had a heap of things to attend to: she had to see to the administration of her farmland and then there was charity work and suchlike.

It was already late September when he walked in through the door one morning. We were happy to see him, so happy that it no longer seemed important whom he had married. Here he was, sitting in the kitchen once more with his curly head and white teeth and deeply-cleft chin and big hands. He stroked the cat and said that he would like to take it away with him: there were mice in the cellar of the house and the cat would learn to kill and eat them instead of being afraid of them as he was at present. He stayed a while and had to have some of my mother's home-made tomato sauce on bread because their cook couldn't make it like this. He took the cat with him in a basket but brought it back a few days later: they had put it in the cellar to kill the mice but the mice were so big and the cat was so frightened of them that he had miaowed all night long and kept the cook awake.

The winter was a hard one for us: Clara's little boy was constantly unwell; he had, it seemed, something seriously wrong with his lungs and the doctor prescribed a substantial, nourishing diet. And we also had the continual worry of the debt towards my father's brother which we were trying to repay a little at a time. So, although we no longer had to support Valentino, it was still a struggle to make ends meet. Valentino knew nothing of our troubles; we rarely saw him as he was preparing for his exams; he visited us from time to time with his wife and my mother would receive them in the living-room; she would smooth her dress and there would be long silences; my mother would sit very erect in the armchair, her pretty, pale, fragile-looking face framed in white hair that was as smooth and soft as silk; and there would be long silences broken from time to time by her kind, tired voice.

I did the shopping every morning at a market some distance away because this meant a little saving on the purchases. I thoroughly enjoyed my morning walk, particularly on the way there with the empty shopping-basket; the open air, cool and fresh, made me forget all the troubles at home and my thoughts would turn instead to the questions that normally occupy a young girl's mind, wondering if I should ever get married and when and to whom. I really had no idea whom I could marry because young men never came to our house; some had come from time to time when Valentino was still at home, but not now. And the idea that I might marry seemed never to have crossed my parents' minds; they always spoke as if they expected me to stay with them for ever and looked forward to the time when I should be selected for a teaching post and would be bringing in some money. There were times when I was amazed at my parents for their never considering the possibility that I might wish to get married, or even have a new dress or go out with the other girls on Sunday afternoons; but although their attitude amazed me, I did not resent it in the slightest, for my emotions at that time were neither profound nor melancholic and I was confident that sooner or later things would improve for me.

One day as I was returning from the market with my basket, I saw Valentino's wife; she was in a car and was driving herself. She stopped and offered me a lift. She told me that she got up at seven every morning, had a cold shower and went off to attend to her agricultural interests: she had a property some eighteen kilometres outside town. Valentino, meanwhile, stayed in bed and she asked me if he had always been as lazy as this. I told her about Clara's child who was sick and her expression became very serious and she said that she had known nothing about this: Valentino had only mentioned it in passing as a matter of no great importance and my mother had said nothing at all about it. 'You all treat me as a complete outsider,' she said. 'Your mother can't stand the sight of me — as I realized the first time I came to your house. It never even occurs to you that I could help when you have problems. And to think that people I don't even know come to me for help and I always do everything I can for them.' She was very angry and I could think of nothing to say; we were outside our flat by now and I asked her, rather timidly, if she would like to come in but she said she preferred not to visit us because of my mother's dislike for her.

But that very day she went to see Clara; and she hauled Valentino — who hadn't been to see his sister for some time, ever since she had called him a pig — along with her. The first thing that Maddalena did on arriving was to open wide the windows, saying that the place smelt dreadful. And she said that Valentino's couldn't-care-less attitude towards his family was disgraceful, while she who had no family of her own found herself getting emotionally involved with the problems of perfect strangers and would willingly go miles out of her way to be of help. She sent Valentino off to fetch her own doctor and he said that the child should be in hospital and she said that she would pay all the expenses. Clara packed the child's suitcase in a state of alarm and bewilderment while Maddalena bullied and scolded her, making her more con-fused than ever.

But once the child was in hospital we all felt a great sense of relief. Clara wondered what she could do to repay Maddalena. She consulted my mother and together they bought a big box of chocolates which Clara took to Maddalena; but Maddalena told her that she was an idiot to spend money on chocolates when she had so much to worry about, and what foolishness was this about repayment. She said that none of us had any idea about money: there were my parents, struggling to make ends meet and sending me off to a market miles away in order to save a few lire when it would have been so much simpler had they asked her to help; and here was Valentino who didn't give a snap of his fingers but was always buying himself new clothes and prancing about in front of the mirror and making a fool of himself. She said that from now on she would make us a monthly allowance and would provide us with fresh vegetables every day so that I would no longer have to trail across town to the market, because her own farm yielded more vegetables than she could use and they simply rotted in the kitchen. And Clara came to beg us to accept the money; she said that after all the sacrifices we had made for Valentino it was only right that his wife should give us a bit of help. So once a month Maddalena's steward arrived with the money in an envelope, and every two or three days a case of vegetables would be left for us at the caretaker's flat and I no longer had to get up so early to go to the market.

My father died at the end of the winter. My mother and I had gone to the hospital to visit Clara's little boy, so my father was all alone when he died. We found him already dead when we got home; he had lain down on the bed and had dissolved some of his tablets in a glass of milk, presumably because he had felt unwell, but hadn't drunk the mixture. In the drawer of his bedside table we found a letter addressed to Valentino which he must have written some days before, a long letter in which he apologized for having always believed that Valentino would become a man of consequence; there was, indeed, no necessity for him to become a man of consequence, it would be enough if he became a man at all, because at present he was merely a child. Valentino and Maddalena came and Valentino cried; and Maddalena, for the first time, was sweet to my mother, showing great tact and kindness; she phoned her steward and asked him to see to all the funeral arrangements and stayed with my mother all night and throughout the following day. When she had left, I remarked on her kindness but my mother said that even when she was kind she couldn't

22

bear her and shuddered every time she saw her beside Valentino; and she said that she was sure that this was the cause of my father's death, his grief at Valentino's having married for money.

Maddalena had a baby in the summer and I believed that this would soften my mother's heart and that she would become fond of the child; I fancied I could see a tiny dimple in the baby's chin and that he looked like Valentino. But my mother denied that there was even a shadow of a dimple; she was very sad and depressed and kept thinking about my father and regretting that she had not shown him more affection; she had never had the patience to let him finish what he was saying but always shut him up and humiliated him. Only now did she realize that my father was the best thing that had ever happened to her in her life; she had no complaints about Clara and me, but still we didn't keep her company as much as we should; and Valentino had married that woman just for her money. She gradually ceased to give piano lessons because she had arthritis and a great deal of pain in her hands; and anyway, the money in the envelope that the steward delivered each month was sufficient for the two of us. When the steward came I always received him alone in the dining-room; my mother stayed in the kitchen with the door shut and never allowed me to mention the envelope; yet this was the money that fed us every day.

Maddalena came to ask me if I would like to spend August with them near the sea. I should have loved to accept but felt I should not leave my mother alone, so I refused. Maddalena told me that I was a fool and a stay-at-home and could rest assured that I should never find a husband. I told her that I didn't care if I never found a husband; but it was untrue, and August was a long, dreary month. Every evening I took my mother out for a breath of cool, fresh air and we would walk through the tree-lined roads or beside the river with her long, slender hand, now deformed by arthritis, resting on my arm and a yearning in my heart to be able to stride out alone and speak to someone who was not my mother. Then she began to keep to her bed all day because her back ached, too, and she complained ceaselessly about it. I begged Clara to come as often as possible but she always had stacks of addresses to type for the company that employed her. She had sent the children away to the countryside for a holiday, including the one who had been so ill but had now recovered; all week long she typed away furiously at her addresses and on Sunday she visited her children. So I was alone in the house when my mother died on the Sunday of the mid-August holiday. All through the night she had complained of the ache in her bones; she was delirious and thirsty and got cross with me for being slow to bring her glasses of water and to plump up her pillows. In the morning I fetched the doctor and he said that there was no hope. I sent off a telegram to Valentino and another to Clara in the country but by the time they arrived my mother was already dead.

I had loved her very much. I would have given anything now to be able to repeat those evening walks that had bored me at the time, with her long, slender, deformed hand resting on my arm. And I felt guilty for not having shown her more affection. I remembered the times when I stood on the balcony eating cherries and heard her calling me but didn't turn round and let her call and call while I hung over the railing and pretended not to hear. I hated the courtyard now, and the balcony and the four empty rooms of the flat; and yet I wanted nothing and had no desire to leave the place.

But Maddalena came and asked me to go and live with them. She was very sweet to me, just as she had been to my mother when my father died: full of kindness and caresses and not at all authoritarian. She said I was free to do as I liked but it was hardly sensible to stay in the flat alone when there were so many rooms in her house where I could get on quietly with my studies and when I felt sad they would be there to cheer me up.

So I left the house in which I had grown up and which was so familiar to me that I could hardly conceive of living any-where else. As I was tidying the rooms before I left, I discovered in a trunk all the letters and photographs sent to Valentino by the teenage girls he used to date, and Clara and I spent an afternoon reading the letters and laughing over them before we burnt them all on the gas stove. I left the cat with the caretaker, and when I saw him again a few months later he had learnt to kill mice and had grown into a big, strong, self-possessed animal, not in the least bit like the wild, timid kitten who had raced up the curtain in fright.

In Maddalena's house I had a room with a big, pale blue carpet. I loved the carpet, and every morning when I woke up the sight of it gladdened my eyes and when I walked on it with bare feet it felt warm and soft. I should have liked to stay in bed for a little while in the morning, but I remembered that Maddalena despised late risers and I could, indeed, hear her ringing the bell furiously and giving orders for the day in her imperious voice. Then she went out in her fur coat and hat squashed to one side, yelled again at the cook and the nurse-maid, climbed into the car and slammed the door.

I went to fetch the baby and dandled him for a while in my arms. I had grown very fond of the child and hoped that he was growing fond of me too. Valentino came down to break-fast yawning and unshaven; when I asked him if he intended to sit for his exams he changed the subject. The steward Bugliari, the same man who used to bring the envelope to the flat when my mother was alive, soon arrived; and a cousin of Maddalena's whom they called Kit would come too. Valentino would play cards with them, but as soon as Maddalena's car was heard in the drive the cards would be hastily hidden because Maddalena didn't like Valentino to waste his time at cards. Maddalena always arrived tired and dishevelled, her voice husky from shouting at the farm workers, and she would start to argue with the steward, pulling out files and ledgers and discussing business at some length. I was con-stantly amazed that she neither asked after her child nor went to see him: the baby hardly seemed to matter to her; when the nursemaid brought him to her she would cuddle him for a moment and while the moment lasted her face became young, gentle and maternal, but then she would sniff the baby's neck

25

and complain that he didn't smell clean and hand him straight back to the nursemaid to be washed.

Kit was a man of forty, tall, thin and slightly balding. The sparse hairs at the back of his neck were long and damp and looked like those of a new-born baby. He had no definite work, and although he owned some land adjacent to Maddalena's he never went there and relied on Maddalena to keep an eye on it; she was always complaining about having quite enough work of her own without being saddled with the responsibility for Kit's land as well. Kit spent every day with us; he played with the baby, chatted to the nursemaid, played cards with Valentino and sprawled in an armchair, smoking. Then, towards evening, he and Valentino would go into town and sit outside a bar watching the elegantly-dressed women as they passed by.

I was very worried about Valentino because he never seemed to study. He would go to the room where he kept his microscope, his books and a skull, but was incapable of sitting at his desk for a minute without ringing down for an egg-flip, and then he would put a lighted candle inside the skull, darken the room completely, call the maid and frighten her out of her wits. Since his marriage he had sat two of his exams and passed them both; he seldom failed an exam because he had a way with words and could bluff examiners into thinking that he knew much more than he really did. But there were still many more exams to go before he qualified and several of his friends who had begun their studies at the same time as he did had been qualified for quite a while. Whenever I mentioned the subject of exams he shied away from it and there was nothing I could do. When Maddalena got home she always asked him if he had been studying and he said yes and she believed him; or maybe she was just tired after spending the whole day working and talking business and preferred to avoid arguments at home. She would sit on the settee with her feet up and Valentino sitting near her on the floor. I found her abject manner towards Valentino embarrassing at these times; she would take his head between her hands and stroke it, and

26

her face shone and her expression became gentle and maternal. 'Has Valentino been studying?' she would ask Kit, and he would reply: 'Indeed he has.' And she would sit there quietly with her eyes closed, stroking Valentino's forehead with her fingertips.

Maddalena had another baby and we went to the coast for the summer. She bore her children with no difficulty at all and continued to go back and forth between the house and her farm throughout the pregnancy; then, once they were born, she found a wet-nurse and had little more to do with them; it was enough for her to know that they were there. She had a similar attitude towards Valentino: she was content to know that he was there but she spent her days apart from him; it was enough to find him at home when she returned, to caress his hair for a while and lie on the settee with his head in her lap. I recalled his telling my mother that with Maddalena he could talk about anything, yet I never noticed them talking at all. Meanwhile, there was always Kit; he was always the one who did the talking, relating endless boring anecdotes about his housekeeper who was simple-minded and nearly blind, or moaning about his bad health and his doctor. And if Kit were not there, Maddalena would ask one of us to telephone and tell him to come at once.

So we went to the seaside, and Kit and Bugliari and the maid and the wet-nurse came too. We stayed in a hotel, a very smart hotel, and I was ashamed of my scant wardrobe but was unwilling to ask Maddalena for money and it did not occur to her, apparently, to offer it; nor did she trouble to look elegant herself but always wore the same sun-dress with blue and white spots; and she said that she had no intention of spending money on clothes because Valentino already spent so much on his. Valentino certainly dressed well, sporting linen trousers and a constant succession of sweaters and tee-shirts. Kit advised him in the matter of clothes even though he himself always wore the same slightly shabby trousers with the excuse that he was so unprepossessing that clothes gave him no pleasure. Valentino went off sailing with Kit while Maddalena, Bugliari and I waited on the beach; and Maddalena said that she was already bored with this way of life because she was incapable of sitting idly in the sun. In the evening Valentino and Kit went out dancing. Maddalena suggested that they might take me with them but Valentino retorted that one did not take one's sister to a dance.

We returned to town and I took my teaching diploma. I was appointed to a temporary post at a school and Maddalena drove me there every morning before going to the farm. I told her that I could live on my own and look after myself now, but she treated the suggestion as an affront and said there was no reason why I should have to fend for myself with such a big house at my disposal and plenty of food to eat; did I really want to rent some tiny room and cook soup over a gas ring? She could see no sense in the idea. And the babies were fond of me and I could keep an eye on them when she was away, and I could also keep an eye on Valentino and make sure that he got on with his studies.

At that point I took my courage in both hands and told her that I was worried about Valentino: he seemed to be spending less and less time on his studies and now Kit had persuaded him to learn to ride and they went to the riding-stables every morning. Valentino had acquired a riding outfit complete with boots, tight-fitting jacket and crop and would stand in front of the mirror at home brandishing the whip and doffing the hat. On hearing this, Maddalena called Kit and gave him a tongue-lashing; she told him that even if he was a failure and a layabout, Valentino was not to become a failure too and he was to leave him alone. Kit listened with his eyes half-closed, his mouth open and one hand gently massaging his jaw; Valentino, meanwhile, angrily retorted that riding was doing him good, that he had been much healthier since he started to ride. Maddalena then ran to fetch the breeches, boots, hat, jacket and whip, parcelled them up and said that she was going to throw them all into the river. She went out with the

28

big bundle under her arm; she was pregnant again and her swollen belly protruded from her fur coat as she ran, limping slightly from the combined weight of her belly and the package. Valentino ran after her and Kit and I were left alone. 'She's right,' said Kit, heaving a deep sigh; he scratched his head with its few straggly hairs and pulled such a comic face that I had to laugh. 'Maddalena is right,' he repeated. 'I'm nothing but a failure and a layabout. She's right. There's no hope for someone like me. But there's no hope for Valentino either: he's just like me, just the same type. Or rather, he's worse than me, because he cares about nothing. I do care a bit about some things; not a great deal, but I do care.' — 'And to think that my father always believed that Valentino would be a man of consequence,' I said. 'Oh really?' said Kit, suddenly bursting into laughter with his head thrown back and his mouth wide open. He rocked backwards and forwards in his chair, clasping his hands between his knees and guffawing. There was something unpleasant in his laughter and I left the room. When I returned he had gone. Valentino and Maddalena did not appear for the evening meal, and there was still no sign of them when darkness had fallen; after I had been in bed for some time I heard them come upstairs and the sound of whispers and laughter told me that they had made it up. The following day Valentino went off to the stables in his riding outfit; Maddalena had not thrown it into the river and the only damage was to the jacket which had got slightly creased and had had to be ironed. Kit stayed away for a few days, but then reappeared, his pockets bulging with socks to be mended which he gave to the maid because he had no one at home to mend his socks, living alone as he did with the old house-keeper who was half blind and incapable of mending anything.

Maddalena's third child was born. It was another boy and she said she was glad that her children were all boys because had she had a girl she would have been scared that it might have grown up to look like her, and she was so ugly that she would not wish that on any woman. She had become reconciled to her ugliness because she had Valentino and the children, but as a girl it had been a source of grief and she had been afraid that she would never get married, afraid that she would grow old alone in the big house with only carpets and pictures for company. Perhaps the reason why she had so many children was in order to forget her previous fears by surrounding herself with toys and nappies and the sound of voices; but having given birth to her children, she had little to do with them.

Valentino and Kit went off on a trip together. Valentino had sat another examination and had passed and said he now needed a little rest. They visited Paris and London because Valentino had never been abroad and Kit said that to know nothing about the great capitals of the world was a disgrace. He criticised Valentino's provincial background saying that it had to be corrected and Valentino must visit dance-halls and famous art galleries. I taught every morning and in the afternoon I played with the children in the garden; and I tried my hand at making toys for them with rags and sawdust as Valentino used to do for the caretaker's children. When Maddalena was out the maid and the cook came to sit with me in the garden; they said that they were not in the least bit shy with me but were very fond of me; and they took off their shoes and put them on the grass beside them, and they made themselves paper hats and read Maddalena's newspapers and smoked her cigarettes. In their opinion I was too much alone and cut off from the rest of the world, and they thought that Maddalena should take me out and about a bit; but all she thought about was her farm. And they said that if things went on like this, I should never find myself a husband: no one ever came to the house apart from Kit and Bugliari; Bugliari was too old for me so they decided that I should marry Kit: he was a nice man but so disorganized, roaming about the city half the night instead of going to bed; and perhaps what he really needed was a woman to look after him and mend his socks and care for him generally. But they were both scared stiff of Maddalena and as soon as they heard her car approaching they put their shoes on and slipped back to the kitchen as quickly as possible.

I visited Clara from time to time but she always made me feel unwelcome and complained that I cared nothing about her or her children any more but only thought of Valentino's boys. All that Maddalena had done for her child when he was ill, arranging for him to go into hospital and paying all the expenses, had already faded from her memory; she no longer had a good word for Maddalena and said that Valentino's marriage to her had completely ruined him: everything was provided for him and we could wave goodbye to our cherished hopes of seeing him qualified. He would fritter away the whole of his wife's fortune eventually. While she spoke she continued to type out addresses; the work had given her corns on her fingers, she had continuous pain in her back and hardly slept at night for toothache. She needed treatment but it was very expensive and she couldn't afford it. I suggested that she ask Maddalena for a loan but this made her indignant and she said she refused to ask favours from people like that. So I got into the way of handing over my stipend to her every month; after all, I had food to eat and a bed to sleep in and wanted for nothing. I hoped that this would make her happier, that she would see a dentist and not tire herself out so much by typing addresses. In the event she continued to type addresses and did not go to see a dentist: she told me that her daughter had needed a new coat and her husband a new pair of shoes and that I had no idea what her life was like but if I ever got married I would find out for myself what a bed of roses marriage really was. Because I, she was convinced, if I got married at all, was bound to land myself with a man without a penny to his name as she had done and after all as a family we already had Valentino who had married money and could hardly expect a second stroke of fortune like that. Speaking of which, it looked like a stroke of luck but in reality was the opposite, because for Valentino having money only meant that he could slouch around doing nothing and frittering it all away bit by bit.

Valentino and Kit returned and we all left for the coast; but Valentino was in a very bad mood and he and Maddalena quarrelled continually. Valentino drove off alone every morning without saying where he was going; and Kit spent the day under the beach umbrella with us and was very unhappy. Half way through August Valentino announced that he was tired of the sea and wanted to go up into the Dolomites: so we went to the Dolomites, but the weather there was wet and the youngest child became feverish. Maddalena blamed the child's illness on Valentino because he had dragged us away on the spur of the moment from the coast where we had been perfectly content to a hotel that was uncomfortable and where you couldn't find a corner out of the draught. Valentino retorted that he could just as well have come alone: he hadn't asked us to come with him but he couldn't move a step without our dogging his heels and he was fed up with babies and nursemaids and the whole lot of us. Kit drove off in the dark to fetch a doctor, and when the child had recovered he went home.

All at once the relations between Maddalena and Valentino seemed to have deteriorated and there was never a moment of peace when they were together. Maddalena was very tense and irritable and as soon as she got up in the morning she began to shout at the maid and the cook. She was irritable with me, too, and snapped at me every time I opened my mouth. And I heard her and Valentino quarrelling loudly late into the night: she would tell him that he was a layabout and a failure just like Kit, but that whereas Kit was a decent person, he, Valentino was not: he was an egoist who never thought of anyone but himself and he was throwing away money on clothes and on other things that she knew nothing about. And Valentino shouted back at her that it was she who had ruined him, that her shouting in the morning was driving him mad and that to see her sitting opposite him at table made him shudder. Sometimes they made it up, Valentino crying and asking her to forgive him and she asking his forgiveness too; and for a while everything was as peaceful as before: he would sit on the carpet and she would lie on the sofa stroking his hair, and they would send for Kit and listen to all his gossip about the town. But these interludes never lasted very long and became increasingly rare: there was many a long-drawn-out day of grim faces and silence succeeded by an outburst of raised voices late at night.

After one particular scene with Maddalena the maid gave in her notice, and Maddalena asked me if I would go to a certain village near her farm to see if I could engage a replacement from among a list of names that she had been given. She would ask Kit to drive me there. So one morning Kit and I drove off. Driving through the countryside, neither of us spoke for some time; every now and then I glanced at Kit's slightly comic profile with the balding head topped by a little beret and the rather pointed nose. I noticed that he was wearing Valentino's gloves. 'Are those Valentino's gloves?' I asked, to break the silence. He took his hands off the wheel for a moment and looked at them. 'Yes, they're Valentino's. He didn't want to lend them to me: he likes to keep his possessions to himself.' I leant my face against the window and looked at the countryside; and the thought of a whole day of freedom ahead, away from that house and its constant quarrels, filled me with a sense of relief and of peace; and it occurred to me that I had to get away from that place: I no longer enjoyed living there, it was too oppressive; I had even taken a dislike to the pale blue carpet in my room which I had liked so much at first. I said: 'What a splendid morning!' And Kit said: 'Isn't it just! And we shall find a splendid girl and we'll have lunch at a little place I know where the wine is excellent. It'll be a holiday, a little one-day holiday: life must be very trying for you with those two quarrelling all the time and never a moment's peace.' — 'Yes,' I said, 'there are times when it becomes unbearable. I should like to get away for good.' — 'Where to?' asked Kit. 'Oh, I don't know, just somewhere.' — 'We could go away together, you and I,' he said. 'Find some peaceful little place and leave those two to get on with it. I've had enough of them too. Many a time when I get up in the morning I tell myself that I shan't go to the house, but somehow I always do in the end. It's a habit; for years I've been used to dining with Maddalena, it's nice and warm there and they mend my socks. My own house is a hovel: there's a coal-burning stove that doesn't draw properly and one day I shall probably die of asphyxiation; and my housekeeper does nothing but gossip. I should put in central heating. Maddalena comes to my place every so often and tells me all the things I should do to improve it. I tell her that I can't afford the money but she says that I could if I would only manage my property sensibly, selling one plot and buying another; she knows all about it. But I don't want to have to make decisions. Maddalena also says that I should get married, but that's something I shall never do. I don't believe in marriage. When Maddalena and Valentino told me that they were getting married, I spent a whole day trying to dissuade them. I even told Valentino to his face that I could have no respect for him. If only they had listened! But now you see what a mess they're in: always squabbling, always making each other unhappy.'

'Do you really have no respect for Valentino?' I asked.

'No. Do you?'

'I love him, because he's my brother.'

'Loving is another matter. It could be that I, too, love him dearly.' He scratched his head under the beret. 'But I have no respect for him. I've no respect for myself, either; and he is just like me, just the same type. The type that will never do anything positive. The only difference between us is this, that he cares for nothing at all, not things nor people nor anything else. He only worships his own body, his sacred body that has to be cared for daily with good food, good clothes and must be allowed to lack for nothing. But I do care a bit, both about things and people, though there's no one who cares about me. Valentino is lucky: self-love never leads to disappointment; but I'm just a poor unfortunate for whom nobody on this earth gives a snap of the fingers.'

We had now reached the village to which Maddalena had told us to go, and Kit drew up and parked the car. 'Now to find this girl,' he said.

We made some enquiries in the village and someone pointed to a house in the distance, high on a hillside, where they thought a girl lived who might be prepared to work in town. We climbed up a narrow pathway with vineyards on either side and Kit became breathless and fanned himself with his beret. 'It's a bit much,' he puffed, 'to expect us to find their maid for them. Why can't they do their own dirty work?'

The girl was out working in the fields and we had to wait for her to return. We sat in a small, dark kitchen and the girl's mother gave us a glass of wine and some little wrinkled pears. Kit chatted away rapidly in dialect to the woman, praising the wine and asking a hundred and one detailed questions about the work on the farm. I sat sipping my wine in silence, my thoughts gradually becoming blurred: the wine was very strong and all at once I felt happy to be in that little kitchen with the open fields beyond the windows and the taste of wine on my tongue and Kit there with his long legs and his beret and his pointed nose; I found myself thinking, 'I do like Kit, he's such a nice person.'

Then we went out into the sunshine and sat on a stone bench in front of the house, eating the pears and enjoying the warmth of the sun. 'How nice this is!' said Kit. He took my hand and, having removed the glove, examined it. 'Your fingers are just like Valentino's,' he said. He pushed my hand away suddenly. 'Did your father seriously believe that Valentino would become a man of consequence?'— 'Yes,' I replied, 'he did. We went without a great many things so that he could study; life was pretty hard and it was always a struggle to make ends meet. But Valentino always had everything he wanted and my father said that one day we would have our reward when Valentino was a famous doctor making important discoveries.'

'Well, well,' he said. For a moment I thought he was about to start guffawing as he had on the previous occasion when we were discussing the same subject in the sitting room. He rocked backwards and forwards on the bench with his hands clasped between his knees; but then he quickly glanced at my face and his expression became serious again.

'You know,' he said, 'fathers always have peculiar ideas. My father wanted me to be an Air Force officer. An Air Force officer! Me! I can't even go on a switch-back because when I look down I get giddy!'

The girl arrived: she had red hair and thick legs with black stockings rolled down to her ankles. Kit fired an interminable series of meticulous, probing questions at her in dialect; he seemed to have an excellent knowledge of all the skills required by a housemaid. The girl said that she would be happy to enter service; she would make her preparations and be ready to leave within two or three days.

We returned to the village for a meal and then went for a long walk through the streets and out into the fields. Kit was in no hurry to get home. Every courtyard that we passed, he pushed open the door, went through and nosed around; on one occasion an irate old woman chased us away and threw a shoe at us as we fled. We went for a long walk through the fields and vineyards. Kit's pockets were still stuffed with little pears and he gave some to me now and then. 'How nice it is to be away from those two!' he exclaimed repeatedly. 'See how happy and relaxed we are! We really should go away together to some peaceful spot.'

It was dark by the time we got back into the car. 'Will you marry me?' Kit said suddenly. He hadn't switched on the engine and was sitting with his hands on the wheel; the expression on his face was a comical mixture of fear and solemnity, his beret sat askew on his brow and his eyebrows were drawn together in a frown. 'Will you marry me?' he repeated sharply; I laughed and said yes. Then he started the car and we drove off.

'I'm not in love,' I said.

'I know; nor am I. And I don't believe in marriage. But who knows? It could be a good thing for both of us; you're such a calm, sweet girl that I see no reason why we shouldn't be happy. We wouldn't do anything extraordinary, we wouldn't

36

travel all over the place, but we could go on little trips like this one occasionally and look at a village or two and nose around the courtyards.'

'Do you remember the old woman who threw a shoe at us?'

'Oh yes,' he said, 'what a temper!'

'Perhaps I should think about it for a while,' I said.

'Think about what?'

'Whether we should get married.'

'Oh yes,' he said, 'we mustn't rush things. But, you know, this isn't the first time that it's occurred to me. Watching you, I've often thought how fond I am of you. I'm basically a decent sort of chap; I've got some bad faults, I'm lazy and I don't get round to doing things: in my house the chimneys don't draw properly and I don't have them seen to. But basically I'm a decent enough fellow. If we get married, I shall have something done about the chimneys and I'll take an interest in my business. Maddalena will approve.'

When we got back to the house, he opened the car door for me and said goodnight. 'I shan't come in,' he said, 'I'll just put the car away and then go home to bed. I'm tired.' He pulled off the gloves and handed them to me, saying: 'Give these back to Valentino.'

I found Valentino in the sitting room reading *Mysteries of the Black Jungle*. Maddalena had already gone up to bed.

'Did you find a housemaid?' Valentino asked. 'Where's Kit?'

'He's gone home to bed. Here are your gloves,' I said and tossed them to him. 'But aren't you a bit past *Mysteries of the Black Jungle*?'

'Stop talking like a schoolmistress,' he replied.

'I am a schoolmistress,' I said.

'I know; but you needn't talk like one to me.'

My supper had been left on a side-table in the sitting-room and I sat down to eat. Valentino went on reading. When I had finished my meal I sat on the settee next to him. I put my hand on his head. He frowned and muttered something under his breath without raising his eyes from the book.

37

'Valentino,' I said, 'Kit has asked me to marry him. I may accept.'

He let the book drop and stared at me. 'Are you serious?' he asked.

'Quite, Valentino,' I said. He smiled crookedly, as if embarrassed, and moved away from me.

'You're not serious, are you?'

'Indeed I am.'

Neither of us spoke for a while. He continued to smile crookedly; I couldn't look at him because there was something unpleasant in that smile: I couldn't understand what was behind it; I sensed shame and embarrassment but didn't understand why he should be ashamed or embarrassed, nor could I understand what was going through his mind.

'I'm getting on, Valentino,' I said, 'I'm nearly twenty-six. And I'm no great beauty and I haven't any money. And I should like to get married; I don't want to grow old alone. Kit's a nice person; I'm not in love with him but my reason tells me that he's a decent person, unpretentious, sincere and goodhearted. If he wants to marry me, I shall be happy to accept; I would like to have children and a home of my own.'

'Ah yes,' he said, 'I see. But don't go rushing into anything. I'm not the best person to be giving advice. But give it some more thought.'

He got up, stretched his arms and yawned. 'He's a dirty fellow,' he said, 'he never washes properly.'

'But that's not a serious fault,' I said.

'I tell you, he hardly ever washes. It is a serious fault. I don't like people who don't wash. Goodnight,' he said, and patted my cheek. A caress of any kind from Valentino was rare, and I was grateful for it. 'Goodnight, Valentino dear,' I said.

All night long I lay thinking about whether I should marry Kit. I was too agitated to sleep. My mind went back over the day we had spent together and I recalled every detail: the wine, the little pears, the girl with red hair, the courtyards and the fields. It had been such a happy day, and it occurred to me that there had not been many happy days in my life, days of

38

freedom to do as I liked.

The next morning Maddalena came to sit on my bed. 'I hear that you and Kit are to be married,' she said. 'It might not be such a bad idea, actually. You would have been better off with a steadier sort of person: Kit's disorganized and lazy, as I keep telling him; and his health is not too good, either. But perhaps you will manage to change his life for the better. There's no reason why you shouldn't. Of course, you will have to be very firm with him: his house is in a dreadful state; he must put in central heating and have the walls painted. And he must keep an eye on his farmland every day like I do. It's good land and would yield well if he would only take some trouble over it; and you must help too. I expect you're thinking that I should be firmer with Valentino; I do my best to persuade him to study, but we always end up having a dreadful row and things are bad. They're so bad, in fact, that I sometimes think we shall have to separate; but there are the children to think of and I haven't the heart to do it. But let's not think about such miserable things for the moment; you're engaged to be married and this is a time for happiness. I've known Kit all his life, we grew up together like brother and sister; his heart's in the right place and I'm very fond of him and want him to be happy.'

My engagement to Kit lasted for twenty days. For twenty days we toured the shops with Maddalena, looking at furniture; but Kit never decided on anything. These were not particularly happy days: I kept thinking about the day we went to find the housemaid, Kit and I, and expected a return of the happiness we had shared that day; but that happiness never returned. We went round the antique shops, always with Maddalena, and Maddalena quarrelled with Kit because he never made up his mind about anything and she told him that he was missing out on some good bargains. The girl with red hair was now installed at the house; she wore a black dress and a little lace cap and I found it difficult to identify her with the muddy peasant girl we had met that day, yet every time I saw her red hair I recalled the little pears and the wine and the dark kitchen and the stone bench in front of the cottage and the wide expanse of the fields; and I wondered if Kit remembered too. It occurred to me that Kit and I should have been spending some time alone together, but he appeared not to want this and invariably asked Maddalena to accompany us when we went to look at furniture, and when we were in the house he continued to play cards with Valentino as he had always done.

Everyone in the house was happy for me. The cook and the nursemaid were delighted and reminded me that they had always said that Kit and I should get married. I had asked the school for a three months' leave of absence on grounds of health; I rested and played with the children in the garden whenever I was not looking at furniture with Kit and Maddalena. Maddalena had told me that she would provide my trousseau, and she insisted on going to tell my sister Clara about the engagement. Clara had met Kit two or three times and couldn't stand him; but she always found Maddalena very intimidating and dared say nothing to her; she was probably impressed, too, by the fact that I was to marry a landed proprietor and not the penniless nobody that she had always predicted for me.

One afternoon when I was in the garden winding some wool, the maid came to tell me that Kit was in the sitting-room and wanted to see me. I took the wool in with me intending to ask him to hold the skein for me. Maddalena was out and Valentino sleeping, so I thought we might be able to have an hour or two to ourselves.

I found him slumped in an armchair with his long legs stretched out in front of him. He was still wearing his coat and was crushing his beret between his hands; he looked pale and depressed.

'Are you unwell?' I asked.

'Yes; I'm not well at all. I feel shivery. I may be in for a bout of 'flu. I won't hold the wool,' he said, glancing at the skein over my arm and wagging a long forefinger to emphasize his refusal. 'Forgive me. I've come to tell you that we won't be getting married.'

He got up and started pacing up and down the room. He continued to crush his beret in his hands, then suddenly flung it down and came to a stop in front of me. We stood facing each other and he put a hand on my shoulder. His face was that of a very old new-born baby, with the sparse hairs plastered damply to the elongated head.

'I'm deeply sorry that I ever proposed to you. I realize that I can never marry. You're a dear girl, so quiet, so sweet, and I had woven a whole world of fantasy for the two of us. It was a beautiful fantasy but all made up and with no basis in reality. I beg you to forgive me. I cannot marry. I'm terrified.'

'That's all right,' I said, 'it doesn't matter, Kit.' I wanted very much to cry. 'I don't love you, as I told you before. If I'd fallen in love with you it would have been difficult for me; but as things are, it won't be too hard. There's no point in brooding; some things we just have to put behind us and soldier on.'

I turned towards the wall, my eyes brimming with tears.

'I really cannot, Caterina,' he said. 'You mustn't cry over me, Caterina: I'm not worth it. I'm a wreck. I spent the whole night thinking how to break this to you; and throughout these past weeks my mind has been in a turmoil. I hate having to hurt someone as dear to me as you are. You would have regretted it bitterly after a while: you would have come to realize the sort of person that I am, a wreck not fit for civilized society.'

I said nothing but stood fiddling with the wool. 'Now I'll hold the skein for you,' he said, 'now I've got all that off my chest and I'm feeling calmer. On my way here, my head seemed to be spinning; and I didn't sleep a wink all night.'

'No, I don't want to wind the wool now,' I said, 'but thank you.'

'Forgive me,' he said. 'I wish there was something I could do to make you forgive me. Tell me, is there anything I can do that would persuade you to forgive me?'

'You don't have to do anything,' I said, 'really, Kit. Nothing has happened; we hadn't bought any furniture, nothing was really settled. We were only toying with the idea and were only half-serious about it.'

'Yes, yes, only half-serious,' he repeated. 'Deep down, no one really believed us. But we can still have the odd day out together; that day we had was such fun. Do you remember the old woman with the shoe?'

'Yes.'

'No one can stop us going out for the day together. We don't need to be married to do that. We'll do it again sometime, won't we?'

'Yes, we'll do it again.'

I went slowly up to my room. I still had the wool to wind, but all at once the effort seemed too much; it was even an effort to drag myself up the stairs, undress, fold my clothes on the chair and get into bed. I wanted to call the maid and tell her that I had a headache and should not be down for supper; but I didn't want to see the maid, I didn't want to see her red hair and be reminded of that day. I decided that I had to leave the house as soon as possible, the very next day, and never see Kit again. And I thought how even the quality of beauty was lacking in my pain because I was not in love with Kit: I felt only shame, shame that he should have asked me to marry him and then changed his mind. And it seemed to me that my attempts over the past weeks to push into the background those things about Kit which I disliked and highlight the things I liked, learning to reconcile myself to the thought of living with his old-baby face, had all been so much wasted effort, a silly, humiliating waste of effort! And how ridiculous Kit had been, panicking at the thought of actually having to marry me!

When Maddalena came into my room, I told her that Kit and I had come to a joint decision not to get married, and that I wanted to go away for a time. I spoke very quietly and kept my face turned to the wall; I had worked out exactly what I wanted to say and had rehearsed the words to myself; now I recited them by heart, very quietly and slowly and completely without expression, as if recounting events that had happened a long time ago; I had chosen to explain things in this way so that Maddalena wouldn't be angry with Kit and also to spare myself some embarrassment. But in the event Maddalena was entirely unconvinced about the decision having been made by both of us.

'You both changed your minds? No; only Kit changed his mind,' she said, and appeared not in the least surprised.

'We both did,' I repeated in a low voice. 'Both of us.'

'Only Kit,' she said. 'I know him too well. You're not the sort of person to change your mind. Anyway, it's no great misfortune; you'll find someone much better than Kit. He's so disorganized. He'll probably come round tomorrow and propose to you again. I know him. Just forget him; you've seen how muddle-headed and indecisive he is; remember how he couldn't even make a decision about the furniture?'

'I want to go away for a while,' I said.

'Where would you go?'

'I don't know. I want to be alone, I don't mind where.'

'As you wish,' she said, and left the room.

I left early the next morning, before Valentino had even got up. Maddalena helped me to pack, insisted on giving me some money and drove me to the station. She kissed me goodbye.

'Please don't quarrel too much with Valentino,' I said.

'I'll try not to,' she said. 'And you mustn't give way to tears and bitterness. That idiot Kit is really not worth it.'

I went to stay with my aunt Giuseppina, my mother's sister. Aunt Giuseppina lived in the country, in the same village where she had spent her whole working life as a school-teacher. She was retired now and spent her time knitting; the knitting brought in a little money and she lived on that and her pension. I hadn't seen her for many years and I was struck by her likeness to my mother; looking at her white hair gathered into a chignon and her delicate profile, I almost had the impression of being with my mother again. I had told her that I had been ill and needed to rest and she was full of concern for me, taking pains to see that I had everything I needed and preparing my favourite dishes. We went for a walk every evening before supper; she walked very slowly, resting her thin hand on my arm, and it was just like walking with my mother.

Every now and then a letter would arrive from Maddalena, short and concisely informative: she and Valentino were getting on so-so, the children were well, they were thinking of me and looking forward to my return. I told Aunt Giuseppina all about Valentino's children and Clara's children; I found myself repeating the same things over and over again and Aunt Giuseppina repeated the same questions over and over again. She was especially curious to hear about Valentino's wealthy wife and that house of hers with all those servants and carpets; and she was rather surprised that I should have left such a comfortable house and come to stay with her in the poor little village with its muddy streets and so out of the way.

After two months with Aunt Giuseppina, the time when I was due to return to my teaching was drawing near and I wrote to our old caretaker to ask if she knew of a room I could rent, for I had no wish to return to Maddalena's house. I prepared to leave and went with Aunt Giuseppina to say my farewells to all her friends and promise them postcards.

One morning I received a letter from Valentino. It was all blots and disjointed sentences. he wrote: 'With Maddalena life has become impossible for us to stay together. I'm extremely unhappy. Come as soon as you possibly can.' And at the bottom of the page he wrote: 'I suppose you heard about Kit's death.'

I had heard nothing. Kit, dead? I could almost see him lying there, dead, his long legs stiffened by rigor mortis. All this time I had tried not to think about him, because although I hadn't loved him his rejection had been a blow. And now he, Kit, was dead!

I wept. I recalled the death of my father and that of my mother; their faces were receding ever more completely from my mind and I would try in vain to recall the phrases they had used every day. And what of Kit's phrases, what had he said? 'Do you remember the old woman with the shoe?' he had said. 'There's nothing to stop us going out for the day together. I'm a wreck,' he had said, 'unfit for civilized society.'

I said goodbye to Aunt Giuseppina. In the train I re-read Valentino's almost illegible scrawl. Another quarrel with Maddalena, then; but I was used to their rows and it was quite possible that they would have made it up before I arrived. But that phrase: 'I'm extremely unhappy' struck a note which puzzled me: it didn't sound like Valentino at all. And how strange, too, that he, who had a horror of picking up a pen, should have written to me at all!

I had never read the papers during my stay with Aunt Giuseppina because in the first place she didn't buy them and in the second place they were always days out of date by the time they got to her little village. So I had known nothing about Kit's death. But why had Maddalena not written? Anxiety clutched at my heart, I was shivering and felt feverish; and the train was rattling at high speed through the countryside past the places we had seen from the car that day when Kit and I had gone to find the new housemaid and had been so happy; and I remembered the wine, the little pears and the old woman throwing a shoe at us.

I got to the house at four o'clock in the afternoon. The children ran across the garden to meet me and made a great fuss of me. The nursemaid was doing the washing in the scullery, the gardener was watering the flowerbeds; everything seemed perfectly normal. I went up to the sitting room.

Maddalena was sitting in an armchair, her glasses on the end of her nose and a pile of socks beside her to darn. It was unusual for her to be at home at that hour and unknown for her to darn socks. 'Hello,' she said, looking at me over the top of her spectacles. She seemed, all of a sudden, to have grown very old, to be a little old lady.

45

'Where's Valentino?' I asked.

'Not here any more. He doesn't live here now. We have separated. Sit down.'

I sat down. 'You're surprised to find me darning socks,' she said, 'but I find it soothes the nerves. Apart from which, I needed a change; from now on I intend to spend my time darning socks and looking after the children and sitting down a lot. I'm tired of managing farmland and shouting at people and wearing myself out. We've got enough money to live on, and now there's no Valentino to throw it away on clothes and all the other things. As for Valentino, I've told him that I shall make him a monthly allowance; I shall send him an envelope.'

'Valentino will come to live with me,' I said. 'We can rent a couple of rooms. Just until there's a reconciliation.'

She made no reply. She was darning very carefully, her lips compressed and her brow furrowed.

'You may make it up very soon,' I said. 'You've had quarrels before and then made it up. He said in his letter that he was extremely unhappy.'

'Ah, so he wrote to you?' she said. 'What did he tell you?'

'He said that he was extremely unhappy, that's all,' I said. 'That was why I came back at once. And he told me that Kit was dead.'

'Ah, so he told you about it. Yes, Kit committed suicide.' Her voice was cold and distant. Suddenly she put down the sock she was mending, the needle still stuck through it. She snatched off her glasses and stared at me with wide, unfriendly eyes.

'I'll tell you what happened,' she said. 'Kit killed himself. He sent his housekeeper away with some excuse or other, lit the stove in his bedroom, opened the top and shut the flue. He left a letter for Valentino. I read it.'

Breathing heavily, she mopped her face, hands and neck with a handkerchief.

'I read it. And then I went through every drawer in the house. There were photographs of Valentino and letters from him. I never want to see Valentino again.' She suddenly began to sob convulsively. 'I never want to see him again,' she said. 'Never let me see him again. I couldn't bear it. I could have borne anything to do with another woman, no matter what had happened. But not this.' She lifted her head and gave me another hard look. 'And the same goes for you: I never want to see you again. Go away.'

'Where is Valentino?' I asked.

'I don't know. Bugliari knows where he is. We have started separation proceedings. Tell him not to worry, Bugliari will bring him his money every month.'

'Goodbye, Maddalena,' I said.

'Goodbye, Caterina,' she replied. 'Don't come here again. I would rather not see any member of your family ever again. I want to be left in peace.' She had picked up her darning again. 'I shall make sure that you can see the children as often as possible,' she said, 'but not here. I'll make arrangements with the lawyer. And I'll send the money every month.'

'The money is not important,' I said.

'It is,' she said, 'it is.'

I was half-way down the stairs when she called me back. I returned. She embraced me, weeping; not angrily this time, but softly and piteously.

'It's not true that I never want to see you again,' she said. 'Come back to see me, Caterina, darling Caterina!' And I wept too and we stood with our arms around each other for a long time. Then I went out into the peace of the sunny afternoon and went to phone Bugliari to ask where I could find Valentino.

Valentino and I live together now. We share two small rooms, a kitchen and a little balcony that overlooks a courtyard very much like the courtyard of my parents' flat. Valentino sometimes wakes up in the morning with his head full of ideas for some commercial enterprise, and he comes and sits on my bed and juggles with figures and dreams about barrels of oil and ships; and then he complains about father and mother and their having insisted on his studying when his real métier was in commerce. I let him talk.

I teach in school every morning and give private lessons in the afternoon; and when I teach at home I ban Valentino from the kitchen because when he's at home he will insist on wearing a shabby old dressing-gown. I find Valentino reasonably docile and obedient and affectionate, too, and when I get home cold and tired after school he prepares a hot-water bottle for me. He has grown fatter because he no longer plays any sport, and the occasional tuft of white hairs is now visible among his dark curls.

He seldom goes out in the morning but wanders around the flat in his shabby dressing-gown, reading magazines or doing crossword puzzles. In the afternoon he shaves, dresses and goes out. I watch him until he turns the corner; but after that I do not know where he goes.

Once a week, on Thursdays, the children come to visit us. They come with their nanny; the nurse has gone now and been replaced by a nanny. And Valentino makes the same rag and sawdust toys for his own children that he used to make for the caretaker's children, dogs and cats and monsters with lumpy bodies.

We never mention Maddalena. Nor do we speak about Kit. Our conversation is strictly limited to daily trivia, to our food or the tenants of the flat opposite. I visit Maddalena from time to time. She has got very fat and her hair is completely grey; she is an old lady. She occupies herself with her children, taking them skating and organizing picnics in the garden. She seldom visits her farm; she is tired of it and says that she has more than enough money already. She spends whole afternoons at home and Bugliari keeps her company. She enjoys my visits but I have to avoid talking too much about Valentino. With her, as with Valentino, I am always careful to keep the conversation on topics which cannot cause pain. We talk about the children, Bugliari, the nanny. So there is no one to whom I can speak the words that most need to be spoken, about the events which most closely concern our family and what has happened to us; I have to keep them bottled up inside me and there are times when they threaten to choke me.

Sometimes I have a feeling of intense anger towards Valentino. I see him there, mooching about the flat in his tatty dressing-gown, smoking and doing crosswords, he who my father always believed was destined for greatness, he who has always taken from others with never a thought of giving anything in return, he who has never neglected for one day to pamper his curls in front of the mirror and smile at his reflection; he who most certainly did not omit that mirrored smile on the very day of Kit's death.

But I can never remain angry with Valentino for very long. He is the only person left in my life; and I am the only person left in his. So I have to repudiate my anger: I must be loyal to Valentino, I must stay at his side that he may find me there if he chances to look in that direction. I watch him walk down the road when he goes out and my eyes follow him until he has turned the corner; and I rejoice in his beauty, in his small curly head and broad shoulders. I rejoice in his step, still so joyful, triumphant and free; I rejoice in his step, wherever he may go.

SAGITTARIUS

MY MOTHER had bought a house in the suburbs of the city. It was a modest house on two floors, surrounded by a soggy, unkempt garden. Beyond the garden there was a cabbage-patch, and beyond the cabbage-patch a railway line. It was October when she moved, and the garden lay beneath a carpet of wet leaves.

The house had narrow wrought-iron balconies and a short flight of steps down to the garden. There were four rooms downstairs and six upstairs, and my mother had furnished them with the few belongings that she had brought with her from Dronero: the high iron bedsteads, shaky and rattly, with coverlets of heavy flowered silk; the little stuffed chairs with muslin frills; the piano; the tiger-skin; a marble hand resting on a cushion.

My mother brought my sister Giulia and her husband to the house with her, and the eleven-year-old daughter of our cousin Teresa who was to attend the grammar school, a white poodle puppy and our maid Carmela, a sullen girl with untidy hair and bandy legs who was consumed with homesickness and spent every afternoon leaning on the kitchen window-sill, gazing at the misty horizon and the distant hills beyond which, she thought, lay Dronero, her home and her old father sitting on the doorstep with his chin in his hand, cursing and muttering to himself.

My mother had raised the money to buy this house in town by selling off some plots of land that lay between Dronero and San Felice; and she had quarrelled with all her relations, who had been opposed to the sale and the division of family property. But my mother had cherished a dream of leaving Dronero for many years, and immediately after the death of my father she began to think about it, discussing the idea with everyone she chanced to meet and writing letter after letter to her sisters in town asking them to help her find somewhere to live. My mother's sisters, who had lived in town for many years and ran a little china shop, were none too happy about her project and harboured a vague premonition that they might have to lend her some money. Miserly and timid as they were, this thought caused them much bitter anguish, but they knew that they would never find the strength to refuse her. My mother found the house for herself; it took her half an hour one afternoon when she came into town. And immediately after agreeing to buy she charged round to the shop to ask her sisters for a loan because the sale of the land could not possibly realize sufficient for her needs. My mother adopted an air of prickly innocence whenever she had a favour to ask; her sisters had no choice and parted with a sum of money which they had no hope of ever seeing again.

Then my mother's sisters were tormented by another anxiety, that my mother, having moved to town, would take it into her head to help them in the shop. And this premonition, like the first, was duly realized. The day after she alighted in town with the cases, the beds and the piano, my mother had abandoned a dazed and bewildered Carmela in the new house, surrounded by sawdust and straw, and, fur-coated with beret jammed askew over wiry grey hair and cigarette clutched in gloved hand, was pacing about the shop giving orders to the delivery man and dealing with customers. Her sisters dejectedly sought refuge in the stock-room, sighing as they listened to the imperious clatter of her high heels. Long familiarity had made words almost superfluous: a sigh told all. The two of them had been living together for more than twenty years in the dark, old shop frequented by a handful of regular customers, elderly ladies whom they regarded almost as friends and whom they would engage from time to time in little whispered conversations between the glove trays and the tea services. They were genteel and timid and dared not tell my mother that her presence disturbed and irritated them and that they were even a little ashamed of her, of her brusque manner and vulgar, moth-eaten fur coat.

When she got home, sighing wearily and moaning over the lack of system at the shop, my mother threw off her shoes and stuck her feet in the air to massage her calves and ankles because she had been standing around all day, and she moaned about those sisters of hers who still had no idea how to run a shop after twenty years, and here she was having to help them out without seeing a penny for her pains, and she moaned about her own stupid generosity which always made her work herself to a shadow for others with never a thought for herself.

I had been living in town for three years. I was now in my third year at the university reading literature, I shared a one-roomed flat with a friend and gave private lessons. In my spare time I also worked as a secretary in the editorial department of a monthly magazine. So, what with one thing and another, I managed to pay my own way. I knew that my mother had told everybody that her main consideration in moving to town was to be near me, to keep an eye on me and make sure that I dressed warmly and had enough to eat; besides, it was no good for a young girl to be all alone in a big city where all kinds of things might happen to her. As soon as she bought the house, my mother showed me the room she had allocated to me; but I immediately, and quite sharply, told her that I intended to go on living with my friend and had no desire whatsoever to return to the bosom of the family; anyway, the house was too far out of town, a full hour's journey from the centre. My mother had not insisted. I was one of the few people who could actually intimidate her and she never dared to argue with me. Even so, she wanted me to have my own room in the house; I could sleep there whenever it suited me. In fact, I did sleep there sometimes, on a Saturday night. In the morning my mother came to wake me bearing on a tray breakfast consisting of coffee and a fried egg. Convinced that I was undernourished, she watched with satisfaction as I ate the egg. She sat on my bed in a new dressing-gown of flaming red silk, her hair in a net and her face smothered with a cream as thick as butter, and told me about her projects. She had any number of projects. She had enough and to spare for the parish poor. This was an expression she often used. Firstly, she wanted to persuade her sisters to give her a share in the shop; because, when all was said and done, it was hardly right that she should slave away for them and never see a penny for her pains. She showed me how her ankles had swollen after standing about at the shop all day. Then she wanted to open a small art gallery. The difference between her gallery and every other gallery in town consisted in the fact that she would offer her visitors a cup of tea every afternoon at five o'clock. She was still debating whether or not to offer little cakes or biscuits with her tea. There was a certain kind of home-made biscuit, delicious but cheap, that one could make with corn meal and raisins. She had plenty of corn meal, in Cousin Teresa's store-room in Dronero. Enough and to spare for the parish poor. And she would ask her sisters to lend her some pretty trays. There were some extremely pretty French-style trays in the shop which nobody seemed to want to buy and it was such a shame to leave them just sitting there gathering dust, and my mother was convinced that the reason her sisters had never made a success of the business lay in their lack of any notion of presentation, and if she managed to set up her art gallery she could turn to good account any number of little things that had been lurking at the back of the stock room since time immemorial: she would set a cut-glass vase of chrysanthemums here, and a china bear holding a table-lamp there, and would steer her visitors' conversation towards the china shop and so drum up business for her sisters who would then have no option but to give her a share in the shop. And as soon as that happened, she would take driving lessons and buy herself a little runabout because she was sick and tired of waiting for trams.

The art gallery, she said, would also be interesting and amusing for my sister and myself, providing an excellent way of meeting people and making new friends. Was she not right, she asked with an enquiring look, in suspecting that my friends were rather few and far between? She had noticed that I seldom went out in the evening and seemed to know no young men. I always looked tired and worried. She would have liked to see a more animated expression, the sort of expression one could expect to see on the face of a young girl of twenty-three with her whole life before her. She was glad that I took my studies seriously and that I was so sensible and level-headed but it would have pleased her to see me with a group of friends, jolly young people to go out and do things with. For example, I never, as far as she could see, went dancing or played any sport at all. I would find it somewhat difficult to get married if I went on like this. Perhaps I hadn't thought much about getting married as yet, but she felt that I was made for marriage and for having lots of children. She looked at me, expecting a reply. Was there no young man who sought my company, no one who interested me a little? I shook my head and turned away from her, frowning and biting my lip. I found these probings extremely distasteful. So she changed the subject and began to examine my petticoat on the chair and picked up my shoes from the carpet to examine the soles and heels. Was this my only pair of shoes? She had found a shoemaker who made shoes to measure very reasonably, and his shoes were quite lovely.

I washed and dressed beneath my mother's attentive gaze. She was unhappy about my grey skirt which I had had for three years, and above all about my dark blue sweater with its baggy, threadbare elbows. How on earth had I got hold of such a garment? Surely to goodness I had something better to wear? And what had happened to those two new dresses that she had had made for me?

Disgruntled, my mother left me and went upstairs to get dressed. She was back in a few minutes to tell me that Giulia and her husband had used up all the hot water for their baths and now she would have to wash in cold water. It wasn't that important, she could have a bath later at her sisters' house, but it was still annoying to be unable to bathe in one's own home. Ah well, it was a relief that Chaim had got round to having a bath for once, though even after a bath he still smelt un-fresh, still had that peculiar odour of mustiness and decay. She failed to understand why he took so little trouble with his appearance. If he was not particularly successful in his profession, the reason undoubtedly lay in his appearance. He would insist on wearing that dreadful old jacket with the leather collar which he could get away with in Dronero but looked positively ridiculous in town. And had I ever noticed his hands? Ugly hands with broken, chewed nails and hair all over them. How unpleasant for his patients, to be pawed with hands like those.

I reminded my mother that Chaim had had many patients in Dronero; in town he was still unknown. Nevertheless, he did have work here, because he had friends at the hospital who recommended him. He had a junior post at the hospital and went there every morning, then, in the afternoon, he visited his patients, chasing all over town from one to the other on his moped. What he needed was a practice of his own in a good central location. My mother had promised to give him the money for this as soon as she had won a certain law-suit against the local council in Dronero, concerning a property dispute; she had made the promise lightly, finding it easy to part with money that was so far away and so unlikely ever to be hers: the litigation had already dragged on for more than three years, and cousin Teresa's husband, a solicitor, had told us that our chances of winning were nil. So the doctor continued to chase all over town on his little moped, in a peaked cap and the old jacket that my mother despised. The truth was that he had no money for a new overcoat: he earned little, and had to hand everything over to my mother for household expenses; he kept back only some change for his cigarettes, and every time he lit a cigarette he got an accusing look from my mother.

My mother's morning routine was unvarying: I knew every gesture by heart. She would sweep to and fro between the bathroom and her bedroom giving orders to Carmela; she brandished her lavender powder-puff, creating a perfumed cloud; licking her index finger, she would draw it along her eyebrows and over her eyelashes, then, peering into the mirror, she would pluck a hair or two from her chin, wrinkling her nose and puffing out her cheeks with a malevolent gleam in her eye; she would smear her lips with a greasy lipstick, pick at her teeth with the tip of a nail, give her woollen beret a good shake, and, pulling a wry face, cram it on her head and secure it with a hat-pin; then, standing in front of the mirror, smoking and humming a popular song, she would slip into her fur coat and turn round a few times to check on her stockings and the heels of her shoes. Then she would leave to go to her sisters, to see what they were having for lunch and whether they had counted the takings.

My sister Giulia sat on a deck chair in the garden, the poodle on her lap and a rug around her legs. She had been ill and had been advised to rest. However, it was my mother's opinion that a life of such total inactivity was doing her no good at all. Both here and in Dronero, both before and after her illness, my sister had never done anything from one day's end to the next. Every now and then she would get up from her deck-chair, fasten the lead on to the dog's collar and walk round the walls of the house with our little cousin Costanza. The life-style of a ninety-year-old, said my mother; how on earth could she work up an appetite? And my mother had still not discovered if Giulia liked living in town or not. She begged me to ask her; she refused to ask her again herself because Giulia's replies were always the same: a flutter of the eyelashes, a shake of the head, a smile. And my mother was heartily tired of this kind of response. Even my own replies were none too satisfactory, she said, and she never knew what I was up to, but at least I had an intelligent face and one could tell some-thing from my expression, whereas poor Giulia was an idiot and her expression told one nothing at all. That little smile of hers made my mother want to hit her. And anyway, what pleasure could Giulia possibly get from living in a town if she

59

never went further than the newspaper kiosk on the corner? The only company she seemed to enjoy was that of the miserable little dog she had bought from a farm-worker in Dronero and our little cousin Costanza. She never went to the cinema and had refused point-blank when my mother had suggested her joining the local cultural society. My mother had joined this society; the members listened to lectures and read magazines.

My sister's marriage had been a profound disappointment to my mother. She had been so confident of Giulia's marrying well. She had taken her on holidays to Chianciano and Salsomaggiore, resorts where my mother could take the waters for the good of her liver and where Giulia could meet eligible young men, and had swallowed glassful after glassful of bitter, tepid water while watching Giulia play tennis, her white dress swirling round her slim legs. The grace of those slender, shapely legs beneath the pleated skirt, the delicate line of the sloping shoulders beneath the thin blouse, Giulia's profile when strands of her hair escaped from her loosened chignon and she raised her white arms to replace the pins, compensated my mother for the intense boredom of a combination of smelly water and the spectacle of a game of tennis. Sipping her water, my mother rehearsed her consent to Giulia's marriage now with one and now with another of the young men leaping athletically around the courts or strolling along the terrace; or she composed the wording of the announcement she would make in Dronero of Giulia's engagement to the extremely wealthy Tuscan industrialist of noble descent who at that very moment was sitting, all unawares, at a nearby table and gazing vacantly before him.

Giulia was soon tired and came to sit down with my mother, her racquet abandoned on her knees and a cardigan flung round the slack shoulders. My mother glanced towards the Tuscan industrialist's table to see whether she could detect a flicker of interest in the vacant eyes. But the industrialist showed no reaction whatsoever and seemed, indeed, not to have even noticed Giulia; suddenly, he waggled a feeble finger in the vague direction of a girl in the distance and made a noise in his throat like the trilling of a bird. My mother decided he was dotty, shrugged a scornful shoulder and dismissed him from the story of her life.

The men were hardly swarming around Giulia, my mother thought, perplexed. Occasionally a young man would show some interest, ask her to dance for an evening or two, sit near her and try to engage her in conversation. But it was not easy to have a conversation with Giulia. A shrug of the shoulders, a flutter of the eyelashes, a smile: this was her conversational repertoire. And how could it be otherwise for the poor girl? She had no interest in the arts, never read a novel and slept through concerts. So my mother tried to fill the void left by Giulia's silence; my mother kept herself up to the minute where modern art and literature were concerned, she belonged to a lending library and even living in Dronero had all the latest books sent to her. No event in art or politics escaped my mother's attention. She had opinions about everything. Even so, the young men would only stay with Giulia for one evening or two at most, then they faded away and my mother would see them, in the distance, chatting and dancing with other girls. But Giulia never seemed to mind. She sat quietly, immobile, her legs tucked neatly beneath her skirt, her fingers interlaced and upon her lips that foolish little smile.

At last, one summer brought a romantic development. The boy was unexceptionable, the match all that my mother could possibly have desired. Giulia had met the boy in Viareggio, where she had gone with cousin Teresa for the month of August. Meanwhile my mother was confined to her bed in Dronero, with a leg in plaster following a fall down the stairs. What with the heat, the pain and irritation of her leg sweating under the plaster, and the letters from cousin Teresa speaking of the probability of an imminent engagement, my mother felt she would really go out of her mind. Twice a day she received a visit from Dr Wesser, who would call to see how her leg was doing and stay to keep her company for a while.

Dr Wesser was a Polish doctor who had sought refuge in Dronero during the war and had chosen to remain. My mother's attitude towards him was a mixture of benevolence and contempt and not for one moment could she have imagined that this skinny little doctor slumped in an armchair chewing his nails and looking about him with a timid smile would one day be her Giulia's husband. My mother's thoughts at that moment were all beating around a beach in Viareggio where even now Giulia might be out on the water in a boat with her young man. She begged Dr Wesser for sedatives to still the twittering of her nerves and demanded to know when she would be able to get up because she was burning with impatience to go to Viareggio and see what was happening. She read Dr Wesser the letters from Giulia and cousin Teresa. Dr Wesser knew Giulia as he had attended her when she had scarlet fever. Giulia's letters were short and clumsy and remarkably lacking in detail; they seemed, observed my mother, like the letters of a seven-year-old writing to Father Christmas. Yet between the sparse lines, pathetically childish though they were, one could discern the glimmer of a tremulous happiness. My mother asked Dr Wesser if there was no way she could scratch her leg under the plaster: it was itching and pricking quite unbearably.

At long last the plaster cast was broken off with a hammer. At long last my mother was able to get up, and within three days she had assembled a holiday wardrobe: spotted skirts, checked skirts, flowered skirts, beach sandals. She felt rather annoyed with cousin Teresa for having written so little about the physique, the family and the finances of the young man. She had confined herself to the statement that this was a good match.

When she arrived in Viareggio, my mother found Giulia in bed with a fever at the hotel, and cousin Teresa sitting beside her applying wet cloths to her forehead. It was nothing to worry about; Giulia had merely caught a slight chill from getting overheated and sitting in a draught. My mother dragged cousin Teresa out into the passage, scolding her furiously and firing a hundred questions at her all at once. Who, for heaven's sake, was this boy? What did he look like? Did he have any money? What was his family like? And why come to a seedy little guest-house like this when they could have chosen a nice hotel?

But cousin Teresa explained that the boy and his parents had transferred themselves to this same hotel a few days ago, having let their own villa. My mother was taken momentarily aback: if these people were having to make do with a small guest-house like this, with its narrow passages smelling of floor-polish and chicken stock, they were unlikely to be enormously wealthy. And, if they were rolling in money, why on earth did they need to let their villa? Cousin Teresa explained that these were well-to-do people of a kind my mother had never before come across: they had a fine old palazzo in Lucca and a holiday villa here in Viareggio complete with bath, refrigerator and garage. The father was a respected judge, the son was also going into law, and he was so much in love with Giulia that he had brought his whole family to stay in the guest-house so that he need never be separated from Giulia for a moment.

In no time at all, my mother was sitting in the garden with the judge, the judge's wife and the boy, fanning herself, smoking and wafting the smoke away from a long ivory cigarette-holder. In her excitement she had almost forgotten all about Giulia lying in bed upstairs with a fever. She talked non-stop, pouring out all the words, the phrases, the speeches that she had had to bottle up through the long lonely seasons in Dronero when darkness gathered outside the windows and the only visitors she could expect, predictable and despised, were cousin Teresa and Dr Wesser. And over the last few weeks, immobile in bed with her leg in plaster, her frustration had been even more acute as she wove fantasies around every letter that arrived from Viareggio and fanned herself and smoked cigarette after cigarette lying back against the pillows and surrounding herself with a host of imaginary people, shadowy, protean forms who smilingly agreed to everything she said. And now here she was, face to face with those who were shortly to become Giulia's new family: an old gentleman, rather dandified in a dark jacket and white trousers; an old lady with a shaky head; and a boy with fair, curly hair who regarded her with a wide grin and an expression of genial wonder and drank fizzy orangeade from the bottle. To these people my mother poured out the story of her life in one steady stream: the death of my father from a heart attack; her years of widowhood, burdened with responsibilities and with the property to administer; the simple, homespun education she had given her daughters; her liver complaint and Dr Wesser's advice; her political opinions, formed by sound common sense and a youthful faith in progress; the difficulties she had had to overcome, living in the country, to keep abreast of contemporary developments in the arts. At times she was nearly overcome by her own emotion: her throat constricted and a sob crept into her voice; at long last she was playing the role she had always dreamt about, that of a mother, full of anxious solicitude, preparing to confide her daughter into the hands of a young man with good intentions, good prospects and a good character. She was so wrapped up in her own performance that she almost forgot to look at the young man in question; later, when she tried to call him to mind, all she could remember was a blond crew-cut and two fleshy lips clamped around the neck of a bottle.

Those few short hours in the garden of the guest-house were the only ones my mother ever passed with the judge's family. During the night my sister began to spit blood, a doctor was called immediately and she was rushed to hospital; three weeks later my mother and Giulia returned to Dronero travelling by sleeper. And nothing more was ever heard of the boy with the blond crew-cut. Cousin Teresa related how the boy's mother had nearly had a nervous collapse when she heard about Giulia spitting blood, and her head had shaken and bobbed about so much that it looked as if it was about to roll off her shoulders; she had insisted upon the family's immediate return to Lucca, tearing the boy away from that guest-house whose very walls seemed to her to be dripping

64

with blood. Cousin Teresa said that as they were leaving, the boy, obviously very upset, had shaken her hand in a corner of the passage with his eyes brimming with tears; but she too had decided to leave at once, frightened and anxious lest she and her daughter, who had slept in the same room with Giulia, might not also be infected.

So my mother was left all alone in the little hospital room with Giulia who lay there, as still and as white as a corpse, with her beautiful hair spread out over the pillow and her lips cracked with fever. My mother was furious with cousin Teresa for leaving her like this, and paced up and down the hospital corridor like a bear in a cage, wearing a spotted skirt now crumpled and dirty because she had too much on her mind to think about changing, even though when it came to skirts she had enough and to spare for the parish poor.

Every time she thought about the boy with the blond crew-cut my mother became enraged. Not one spark of generosity had he shown! No crumb of comfort had he offered! And to think that he had disappeared without even saying goodbye! Without a single word of any kind! The very memory of the blond crew-cut and of the afternoon spent with his family now filled her with disgust. But once the fear for Giulia had begun to subside, and the doctors had assured her that given the resources of modern medicine Giulia would make a complete recovery, once back in Dronero with Giulia installed in the big bed with its flowered silk coverlet, propped up with two plump pillows and with the tonic prescribed by Dr Wesser on the table beside her, my mother, thinking of all the high hopes she had cherished within these familiar walls, began to ask herself precisely what had passed between Giulia and the boy. Had any promises been made? Any undertakings given? She dared not mention the subject to Giulia herself who still lay, weak and wasted, against the pillows, with a little shawl around the white arms veined with blue, her hair tied back with a black velvet ribbon and the usual feeble smile on her lips that conveyed nothing at all. Was she grieving? Who could tell. At night my mother's fancy continued to trip around the city of Lucca and the fine old palazzo where the judge's family lived, with its vaulted ceilings covered with fifteenth-century frescoes which, according to cousin Teresa, would sooner or later become a national museum. She went to see cousin Teresa and plied her with endless questions about those weeks in Viareggio until cousin Teresa begged her to leave her in peace; she had told her everything she knew, the business had ended badly and there was nothing they could do about it.

Nevertheless, throughout the winter my mother continued to wait anxiously for the post, every day more convinced that a letter would arrive from the boy with the blond crew-cut either for Giulia or herself. It never came. Instead, she got a constant stream of letters from a night nurse at the hospital in Viareggio to whom she had imprudently promised a job at the hospital in Pinerolo where a friend of Dr Wesser's worked. But since then my mother had had a slight disagreement with Dr Wesser and had never mentioned the matter to him.

My mother had suspected for some time that Dr Wesser was in love with Giulia. He spent hours and hours with her, translating German poetry for which Giulia patently did not care a fig, and showing her all his family photograph albums full of Polish gentlemen in fur coats and top hats and ladies with long ropes of pearls and plumed headdresses; poor unfortunates murdered during the war, unhappy Jews who had been torn from their beds by the Nazis and herded off to their deaths in some unknown place. Dr Wesser had no family now apart from a younger brother who had left Poland with him and now lived in town, working at a chemical plant; he was the only person left in the world whom Dr Wesser loved. Giulia listened patiently to the doctor's dreary narrations, and to please him she leafed through the albums looking at the pictures of Dr Wesser's parents, a refined and confident couple and how sad to think of them dying like that, probably in one of those freezing camps, breaking stones; and there between them stood the doctor and his brother, small children dressed up as cossacks for some carnival ball.

Giulia was much better now and was able to get up and go for walks. The doctor would accompany her sometimes, pushing his moped and probably telling her more tragic stories about his dead relatives; quite unsuitable for a young girl, thought my mother, becoming more and more irritated with Dr Wesser whenever she saw, from the vantage-point of her balcony window, the tall figure of Giulia flanked by that of the doctor scarcely reaching her shoulder and bundled up in the brown coat given him by the association for Jewish refugees, a three-quarter-length garment with a leather collar and half-belt, neither jacket nor overcoat. My mother thought resentfully of all the favours she had done Dr Wesser; of how, when the Germans had come to Dronero and the doctor had hidden in cousin Teresa's house, she had taken him cigarettes every day; and of how, when he had had colitis, she had given him wool to make a warm stomacher; and she thought of all the bottles of maraschino he had got through on those evenings when he had sat with them around the stove translating the poems of Hofmannstahl for Giulia, '*Hof*mannstahl' scoffed my mother with a shudder, imitating the doctor's heavily-aspirated aitch and the way he fiddled with his tie and smoothed the hair on his temples with little, quick movements as he read. My mother had now begun to treat Dr Wesser badly, always finding some pretext or another: she asked him about a book she had lent him years ago and knew that he had mislaid; she complained that the tonic he was prescribing for Giulia was indigestible; and when he came round to see her one rainy evening, she whisked his wet jacket furiously off the sofa. The doctor picked up his jacket, hung it on a hook and went on reading Hofmannstahl to Giulia in his gentle, monotonous voice.

Sometimes my mother heard the doctor and Giulia laughing together. She had no idea what they were laughing about; and that the doctor could ever have the slightest desire to laugh after all his family tragedies, that he could laugh and play the fool with all the worries he had, with no money and a brother who was often out of work, she found incomprehensible. The doctor had no house of his own but rented a room above the bar, where he cooked his own supper of some Polish hash over a tiny gas-ring and washed his own few items of clothing, hanging them over a line stretched between the bed and the wardrobe to dry. In the wardrobe, among the books and socks, the doctor stored the cheese and eggs that his patients on the outlying farms gave him; he attended everybody, even if they could not pay him, and everybody loved him; even the eggs he was given he seldom ate himself, but gave them to the children he saw playing in the street, saying that growing children needed eggs more than an old man like himself. Not that he was old, not above forty at most, but he carried himself badly and walked awkwardly, with one shoulder higher than the other and shuffling his feet; and when he became friendly with Giulia, he suddenly appeared to my mother to be positively ancient and the most unprepossessing person she had ever seen.

One evening, when Giulia was sitting in an armchair near the stove with a box of oddments of wool on her lap, making multi-coloured dolls for our little cousin Costanza, the doctor told my mother that he and Giulia were planning to get married in the coming spring. My mother had been expecting this for some time, yet the words hit her like a blow in the stomach. She turned to look at Giulia and saw exactly what she had expected: her face was calm and sleepy and wore its usual silly little smile; Giulia was holding a length of wire and twisting a piece of wool around it. She had been doing this for some days now, producing shapeless little dolls that looked like nothing on earth and had no character at all. Did she want to marry the doctor? My mother shouted at her, snatching the box of wools from her lap. Giulia raised her arms as if to fend off a blow and her face flushed bright red. Seeing this, my mother felt a great surge of pity for her; she replaced the box and went to sit in a corner, turning her back on Giulia and the doctor; and from her corner she said yes, by all means go and get married, after all she was old now and nothing mattered two pins to her any more.

The next day my mother went to see cousin Teresa. Yes, cousin Teresa had known about it for some time: Giulia had confided in her. Giulia was certainly not in love; she had never been in love with anybody since the Viareggio affair; but she liked the doctor and was content. She admired him for his learning and refinement, and on the days when he went into town to visit his brother she felt lost and even more bored than usual. Besides, said cousin Teresa, Giulia was now twenty-five. And she had had that dreadful illness which would always make it difficult for her to find a husband because it frightened people. And it was not such a bad arrangement for Giulia, who needed constant medical attention, to have a doctor always on hand to attend to her without payment; and this, said cousin Teresa, flashing all her silver teeth, was a consideration not to be sneezed at.

My mother went to all her female relations, her cousins and her aunts, trying to find someone who would dissuade Giulia from this marriage. But the cousins and the aunts refused to interfere; they shook their heads and said that at long last poor Giulia had found herself a husband and it would have been a great pity had she been left on the shelf; of course, Dr Wesser was neither handsome nor rich, nor was he young, but he was a good man and all the children loved him and ran up to him whenever they saw him. Are you mad? yelled my mother. Do you really want to see Giulia married to a man like this, a Communist, a Jew, a stateless person? The cousins and aunts wagged their heads. Dr Wesser a Communist? Strange, they had never heard that before. But why should it worry my mother if he was a Jew? Had she not always shouted it from the rooftops that the Negroes and the Jews are all our brothers?

Eventually, cousin Teresa gave a dinner to celebrate the engagement. And at the end of dinner, as a splendid cake decorated with glacé cherries was put on the table, cousin Teresa virtually pushed my mother into Dr Wesser's arms and she was obliged to plant a kiss on the bony cheek furrowed with a single, deep line.

My mother now felt a great emptiness within. Her heart,

which had throbbed with so many precious hopes, seemed to have died in her breast. Dronero, too, now seemed drearier than ever; Dronero, where she knew every single stone by heart; Dronero, where every other house harboured a nest of relatives of one kind or another. She longed to live in the big city where there were a hundred things to do and where even a stroll through the street was an amusing experience; and she felt a sudden nostalgia for me, too. It occurred to her sometimes that I might make a good match. I was no beauty like Giulia, of course, and my height, or lack of it, was a defect; my mother could never understand why I should have stayed so short; and my hair was a mass of tight waves forming a frizzy, shapeless cloud around my head. Still, these undoubted defects were compensated by the fact that I was much more intelligent than Giulia, and some day I might even write books, having secretly scribbled verses in exercise books since I was a child. She often came into town, ostensibly to buy things for Giulia's trousseau, and she would arrange to meet me in some coffee-bar and ask me whether I was still writing poetry. She was a bit anxious about my teeth, which were crooked; when I was little, she had wanted me to wear a brace to straighten them, but my father had put his foot down. My father, poor soul, had had his eccentricities. She wondered what we could do about my hair. We were sometimes joined in the coffee-bar by my friend, the girl with whom I shared a flat. My mother was none too happy about two girls living alone, but the serious expression of my friend, who was older than me and taught history in a senior school, reassured her. My mother showed us the things she had bought for Giulia, undoing packages of petticoats and nightdresses at the table and displaying them to my friend; and she asked my friend to help her find somewhere in town because Dronero had become unbearable and she had decided that she simply must move into town. Then she ruffled up my hair again — I pulled my head away — and asked my friend, too, what she thought I ought to do about it. Then she started to tell my friend and myself about Dr Wesser, and a note of something very like pride crept into her voice; she said what an incredibly cultured man he was, speaking sixteen languages, knowing a great deal about music and having read all the philosophers; and she told us about the former wealth of his family back in Poland when he was a boy, how they were one of the best families in Crakow and owned great chests of silver and how his mother, when she went to a ball, wore a diamond tiara.

On the coach returning to Dronero, my mother felt happy and her spirit refreshed after a few hours in town spent shopping and chatting to my friend and me and nosing around her sisters' china shop, and she was impatient to get home and show Giulia, the doctor and cousin Teresa all the pretty hemstitched nightdresses she had been buying, spreading them out triumphantly on the dining-room table.

The doctor met her off the coach to help her with the parcels, and my mother, after her grandiose descriptions of his family's past wealth, now saw him as one embellished, as it were, with the aura of that wealth which, although it had vanished, was still a fact of history, so she felt more kindly disposed towards him.

Totally without warning, one evening when she was in the dining-room with Giulia and the doctor after one of her shopping expeditions, my mother announced that she had bought the house in town. She intended to move into town, she said, because she had wanted to do so for many years and because she was now so bored with Dronero that she wanted to scream every time she looked out of a window. And when they were married, Giulia and the doctor must come and live with her in town because she had chosen a large house expressly and intended that Giulia should never be separated from her. As she spoke, she realized that she was spoiling for a fight; she was expecting the doctor to object, to say that he and Giulia intended to remain in Dronero, and she had her reply all worked out. He was welcome to stay behind in Dronero with Giulia, but Giulia was, of course, used to a very high standard of living and to having every last thing done for her; she would not even stoop to pick up a pin; he would have to be prepared to wait on her hand and foot, prepare little delicacies for her tea and iron her blouses; and the money he earned couldn't even buy the milk for the puppy. She had the very words on the tip of her tongue: 'not even the milk for the puppy'. But the doctor merely replied, as calmly as you please, that he would be very happy to live in town and had had no intention of making a permanent home in Dronero; indeed, for some time now he had been thinking of moving to town to be near his brother of whom he was very fond. So my mother was left seething with frustration and choking on the angry words she had been given no excuse to deliver.

Giulia and the doctor were married in the spring. There was a church ceremony, but because the doctor was a Jew, Giulia had to have a special dispensation from the bishop and the priest was not allowed to make the sign of the cross over the couple. The doctor stood beside Giulia with his shoulder twitching and one hand continually fingering his tie and his Adam's apple. My friend came, too; she, too, declined to make the sign of the cross, because she was an atheist, and she stood looking about her with her habitually serious expression. The doctor's brother was also there, a short, bespectacled young man with freckles, and my mother, her head adorned with a diminutive concoction of blue feathers and her face with many layers of tear-streaked powder. Afterwards, Giulia and the doctor left for a brief honeymoon on the Riviera, and when they returned the doctor piled his books, his gas-ring and his few articles of clothing into a suitcase, and after a long and tearful farewell from his landlady came to live in my mother's house.

By now my mother had got used to calling him by his first name, Chaim; she found it was not unpleasant to pronounce a name so unusual and foreign.

My mother was now busy with preparations for the move and could be heard all day long shouting at the maid Carmela, who should have been packing up the plates but managed to break everything she touched; and Carmela's relatives were always in the house on the pretext of saying goodbye to her, and her old father was installed next to the kitchen stove eating bread and cheese, his beard full of crumbs and his leaky old boots making dirty pools on the floor. And cousin Teresa was there all day long, pestering my mother to leave her various articles such as the rubbish-bin and the wash-tub because it was more nuisance than it was worth to pack up such things and surely it would be better to buy new ones. Cousin Teresa told Carmela to put these things to one side and promised to give her father a nice pair of old slippers in exchange.

Tears came into Carmela's eyes whenever she thought of leaving her old father behind, all alone, in Dronero without a soul who would go to see if he were alive or dead; because no one in the family could be bothered with the old man who was half mad and invariably drunk; and she asked cousin Teresa to ask her husband, the solicitor, to help him get some poor relief, because they had been trying for years but had always been turned down, although there was nobody in Dronero poorer than they were and anyone could see what a poor old man he was.

Carmela had been with our family for a long time, off and on: because every now and then she would be seized with compassion for her father, so old and mad and lonely, and would go back to the wretched hovel at the bottom of a narrow alley-way, a hovel as dark as a cellar and crawling with cockroaches; and she would return after a few days with her father who would beg us to take Carmela back because he got drunk every evening and when he was drunk he beat her up; and he would make Carmela roll up her sleeve and show us the bruises on her arm. My mother would look at the bruises and threaten to go to the police, but then agree to take Carmela back, sighing over the softness of her own heart and all the trouble it let her in for. In fact, my mother was always delighted to have Carmela back, for she paid her almost nothing apart from presents of cast-off clothing.

At night, Carmela's father came to the house, drunk, and sat beneath the balcony whining about his wretchedness and about his only daughter having to work as a servant; then he went on to sing the praises of my mother, a lady with such a soft heart, a true lady. Carmela hid behind the shutters, crying; but my mother lay in bed luxuriating in the sensation of hearing her praises sung in the dark, silent street. So she never turned Carmela's father away when she found him in the kitchen, cosily installed beside the stove, munching bread and cheese. But in the morning my mother complained of a dreadful headache as the result of a disturbed night, and lectured Carmela on all the trouble and suffering she had to bear as the price of retaining her in the house. She even said that one of the main advantages of moving to town was that she would no longer be subjected to these whimpering serenades; and Carmela was completely abashed, thinking that the family was being forced to flee the village on her father's account.

After a few months in town my mother began to show signs of restlessness. She soon tired of her sisters' shop, where the only customers were tight-fisted old women who could haggle for hours over the price of a teacup; and one day, turning round quickly, she knocked over a pierrot playing a guitar. She said that she had never liked the pierrot, that the figurine was probably unlucky and that she was pleased it was broken; besides, it was a cheap and nasty thing in white porcelain with touches of blue, the sort of ornament one only saw at the dressmaker's; indeed, she had a good mind to glue the pieces together and give it to her dressmaker. Watched anxiously by her sisters, she gathered the bits and put them in her handbag. On her way out she airily promised to pay for the pierrot, saying her sisters were lucky because they could never have sold it. Since that day she had taken a dislike to the shop, and her sisters had, anyway, remained unshakable in their determination not to offer her a share. The fragments of the pierrot lay undisturbed in her bag for a while; then she threw them into the dustbin.

There were days when my mother was almost as bored in

town as she had been in Dronero. She already knew the central shopping district like the back of her hand, having walked the length and breadth of it looking for suitable premises, small but attractive, for her art gallery; but the rents were all extremely high and, besides, another problem was beginning to occur to her, that of finding painters willing to show in her gallery. She knew nobody. Before coming to town she had imagined that it would be easy to make acquaintances, to surround herself with people of culture that she would enjoy talking to, but the reality had been rather different. Ever since her arrival in town, the only people with whom she had exchanged more than two words together had been the shoemaker, the corsetière and the dressmaker; and sometimes she would go to see one of these on the mere pretext of taking measurements, scrutinizing materials or studying patterns — which she had no intention of ordering — just for the sake of talking to somebody and having something to do; and she paced up and down in the same way that she did at home, smoking and flicking her ash on the floor; and holding up a length of cloth or a strip of leather to the light, she made comments in a loud voice and slipped in references to her opinions on art and politics and anything else that occurred to her, hoping that other clients, specifically any client of taste and refinement, would overhear, admire her spirit and demand to know who she was. But nothing ever happened, and the days dragged by, each one emptier and more aimless than the one before. No visitors came to the house apart from Jozek, Chaim's younger brother, a distinctly unamiable young man who sat in the corner of the dining-room reading Polish novels; and when he spoke he became irritatingly pedantic, delighting in the expression of opinions contrary to my mother's. Now and then he would enquire with a sarcastic smile about the art gallery, asking if she had found a place for it and if the opening would take place soon. Incensed, my mother snapped at him, telling him to mind his own business; and Chaim, with his gentle smile and twitching shoulder, tried to restore the peace. Giulia sat in the rocking-chair with the puppy on her lap, Costanza sat at the table doing her homework and Jozek teased her by pulling off and pocketing her hair-ribbon; Costanza screamed and tried to kick him. Supper-time approached and Jozek showed no sign of leaving; he was hoping my mother would invite him to stay and dine with them, but my mother, out of pique, intended to do nothing of the sort: she glanced pointedly at her watch and went round plumping up the cushions. Finally, the doctor said something in Polish to his brother, probably suggesting that he should go; and Jozek went, throwing Costanza her ribbon as he went; and Carmela appeared, her face always gloomy and bad-tempered, her gait clumsy and pigeon-toed, and put the tureen on the table.

My mother still thought about her art gallery occasionally, but had projected it into an ever more dim and distant future and her ideas about it had become ever more pale and blurred. And when she compared her lively fantasies of the past with her monotonous existence, she felt herself to be the victim of some great injustice. She was unclear as to whom to blame for this injustice, but vaguely attributed it to her own lack of money, to Dr Wesser's earning so little and to Giulia for having married him; and she became irritated with Carmela who was stupid and dirty and left her filthy aprons draped over the armchairs, and with Costanza who was extravagant with the jam, and with cousin Teresa who didn't pay enough for her daughter's keep. Cousin Teresa had originally intended her daughter to live with the nuns while she was at school; it was my mother who had insisted on looking after the child because she thought a convent would be too dreary a place for the young girl; now she was beginning to understand what a responsibility she had undertaken; but that was her nature, always to take the burdens of others upon her own shoulders with never a thought for herself, and it never brought her anything but trouble.

She spent hours walking aimlessly about the town, looking at shop windows and muttering about the increasing prices; then she sat down wearily in some coffee-bar, fitted a Turkish cigarette into the long ivory holder, ordered a coffee granita with cream and looked around her, smoking and feeling cross with Giulia who could never be persuaded to leave the house. I was at least studying for a degree, but Giulia did nothing but sit by the window with the puppy in her arms, gazing out beyond the garden to where the trains were passing in the fog. Giulia's was a senseless existence. Towards evening the place began to fill up and my mother tried to eavesdrop on the conversations around her; these conversations always struck her as fatuous, but even so she would have been more than happy to join in; but where were all the cultured people, the intellectuals, the writers and painters, those to whom my mother was planning to offer cups of tea in her gallery? She had attended a few meetings at the literary club, but even here she had been disappointed: the lectures were infrequent and dry and only attended by a few old people who fell asleep in the middle. My mother had been to one lecture on a composer called Béla Bartók; the name sounded suspiciously Polish, and from the Poles, according to my mother, one could hardly expect anything of quality. On another occasion a slender, pretty young man with a tiny button nose had flitted about the room on the tips of his toes, reading extracts from a novel about a whale; the whale had been very boring and all the little old people around her had dozed off, but my mother endured to the end, sitting motionless in the front row and fixing the youth with her bright black eyes. Seen close up, the youth had the face of a worn forty-year-old, like a rosy fruit pinched by the frost. But the youth, the little old people, the room and the whale did not, it seemed to my mother, add up to real culture. Where, then, was real culture to be found? Where were the real intellectuals? Where were they hiding? In their absence my mother found the town empty and boring.

Sometimes my mother came up to my little flat. She brought a little box of cream cakes with her, partly because she had a weakness for them and partly because she felt guilty for having scoffed a coffee granita with mountains of whipped cream all by herself. Finding me at my studies, she opened the box on

77

my desk and went to fetch a plate from the kitchen. She tended to laugh at our tiny kitchen the size of a cupboard, but she said that a little flat like this with just one room, bathroom and kitchen, would have done just nicely for her too; she was tired of running a big house and catering for so many people morning, noon and night, and above all she was tired of Chaim. I asked her what she had against Chaim who was so kind and polite and self-effacing; but she told me I would never understand and she frowned and rattled the big pearls of her necklace against her chest. To distract her, I said how pretty her necklace was; only a cheap trinket, she said, picked up for next to nothing. We heard the sound of a key turning in the lock of the front door and my friend came in, unbuttoning her mackintosh and pushing back the short, wet strands of hair from her forehead. Her fiancé, an engineering student, was with her. While my friend prepared some tea, my mother observed her fiancé who was a tall young man with a fresh complexion and ears that stuck out almost at right-angles. We all had tea together and finished off the cakes; then my mother began a conversation, but almost at once my friend and her fiancé said that they would have to go: they were to be married within two or three months and had to see about some furniture.

When we were alone again, my mother pronounced upon the young man: a fine-looking boy, pity about the ears; how extraordinary that my friend should have acquired such a good-looking man, for she was no beauty herself, poor dear; a nice girl, certainly, but positively no beauty. My mother wanted to know if I would return to live with her once my friend was married, but I replied that I would be staying on in the flat with its tiny kitchen; it belonged to my friend and I would only be paying a very low rent; when she was married, my friend and her husband were going to live in a flat owned by his father. Well well, said my mother, so they were people of property and my friend was marrying into money; some had all the luck, while everything she did seemed fated to turn out badly: she was born under an unlucky star.

Before she went, my mother said, with a deep sigh, how

sorry she was to be going because I was the only person she enjoyed being with; Giulia was no company at all because they had nothing left to say to each other, nor, to tell the truth, had they ever had much to say to each other. Sighing, my mother did up her fur coat and put on her scarf; and she stowed the cardboard tray that had come with the cakes into her handbag because Carmela could grate the cheese on to it.

My mother met Signora Fontana at the hairdresser's. My mother was sitting in the main salon because all the cubicles were occupied; she was under the drier with a pile of magazines on her lap. Space was restricted, so they had put her in a corner near the door; this door opened on to a courtyard and every time someone opened it she felt a blast of cold air. Under the hood, her head was feeling not only dry but baked and the pins were like red-hot needles; and what with the heat of the drier and the blasts of cold air from the door, she was sure she would get pneumonia. She called out, complaining that she had had enough and would someone come and comb her out, but no one paid any attention; the girls bustled to and fro, gave her head a quick prod and told her to get back under the hood. Seated on a high swivel-chair next to my mother was a short woman with a shock of straw-coloured hair, a pointed face and myopic eyes; her skin was porous and the colour of putty and she was holding her hands in the air and waving them about to dry the nail-varnish. She too was complaining about the draught and she began to sympathize with my mother for being left for so long under the drier, laughing about it in a rather insolent manner. She explained that she only came to that place to have her nails done because she did her own hair at home now that her daughter had given her a hair-drier for her birthday.

The woman had a hoarse, strident voice and was wearing an unappealing dress in a black and white check and sandals much too light for the time of year. My mother, for once, was disinclined for conversation; she had taken offence at the way

79

this little woman with the shock of hair had laughed at her when the assistants had ignored her, so her first replies to the woman's observations were cold and monosyllabic. But the little woman chattered on, saying how the salon had gone down lately, how overcrowded it was and how the girls were always so rude and inattentive; one of them had once been in such a hurry that she had spilt a bottle of some chemical all over her daughter's new red dress, and they had had to have it dyed black which was quite the wrong colour for a young girl of eighteen.

She told my mother that she had known her by sight for some time, having seen her at the shoemaker's. They had the same shoemaker, she said, holding up her sandal-shod feet, and he was really first-rate: his shoes were so soft you hardly noticed them on your feet. She only ever wore sandals, she said, because her feet were very sensitive and she hated to feel them enclosed; when it was wet she wore synthetic-rubber galoshes, very light-weight, like American women wore nowadays. But when it was cold? asked my mother. Did she not get chilblains when it was cold? The little woman laughed. She had never had a chilblain in her life, she said, because she had excellent circulation; she never wore a hat or gloves, either, but if she did wear a hat, she got a cold immediately. She was sure she was going to get a cold now, because although cold weather never affected her, she was susceptible to draughts and this salon was certainly draughty. As soon as she got home she would get herself a nice glass of hot milk laced with rum.

They left together and the woman suggested going some-where for a coffee. She said her name was Priscilla Fontana but her friends called her Scilla; she was separated from her husband, had one daughter and worked as a designer for a fashion house; she also painted in her spare time. My mother now began to take more interest in this strange little woman with her slightly insolent manner; she looked at the small, sandal-shod feet, the rather shabby fawn wool coat, the shock of blond hair blowing in the cold wind and rather wished that

80

she too was wearing sandals instead of patent-leather stilettos.

They found a table at the coffee-bar and sat down. Signora Fontana had arranged to meet her daughter there but as yet she had not arrived. My mother would have liked a coffee granita with cream, but dared not order it in case Signora Fontana intended to pay; so she ordered something much cheaper, a small vermouth, and Signora Fontana ordered a *rabarbaro* with a slice of lemon and a drop of bitters. My mother was now anxious to talk about her gallery project but was unable to get a word in edgeways because Signora Fontana never stopped chattering for an instant. She was sitting opposite my mother with her elbows on the table and her pointed chin cupped in the palm of one hand, and talking so fast that my mother could hardly follow her; about Barbara, and Gilberto, and Menelao, all people my mother did not know. Then she discovered that Menelao was a cat. She felt tired and confused and her head was in a whirl; and she was feeling slightly bored, too, as always happened when someone else was doing all the talking.

Then she discovered that Barbara was the daughter; and eventually Barbara herself appeared. She was beautiful, and my mother was astonished because she had certainly not expected this faded little woman to have a beautiful daughter. Barbara walked towards them slowly, tossing a thick pony-tail of flaming red hair from side to side; she had a round, rosy face, very small, white teeth and wide-set eyes. She was wearing an amply-cut overcoat with the belt hanging loose and a bright green scarf that made her complexion look positively dazzling and was carrying a school satchel under her arm. All heads turned as she walked by, and my mother suddenly felt very unhappy: she had always thought Giulia was beautiful, but now that she had seen Signora Fontana's daughter she had to concede that there was no comparison. What, after all, were Giulia's claims to beauty? Giulia had never turned a single head, and even if she were beautiful, what good had it done her, seeing that she had married Dr Wesser? For a few moments while Barbara sat down at their table, undid her scarf and ordered a strawberry ice smothered in cream, my mother's thoughts were bitter; then, as she studied Barbara more closely, she noticed that she had a few freckles, a slightly snub nose and breasts that were too large; at thirty those breasts would droop, anything could happen to those breasts by the time she was thirty.

Even so, when my mother reached home that evening, she was feeling discontented with herself and all around her and wished that she were returning not to her own home but to the little sixth-floor flat in Via Tripoli where Signora Fontana lived, to find the cat Menelao waiting for her and an old maidservant called Settimia, so devoted that she refused to accept wages; but, despite her protests, Signora Fontana had opened a savings account for her. There were always four or five people round the table in Via Tripoli, because whenever anyone came to call they were automatically invited to stay for a meal. It could be Gilberto, Signora Fontana's ex-husband, who dropped in, for although legally separated they were still the best of friends. Gilberto was in the retail business, and when things were going well would bring her gardenias and boxes of chocolates; or it might be Crovetto, a friend of Gilberto's who went shooting and always brought her quails or partridge, and no one knew how to prepare quails and partridge better than Settimia. Another guest might be Pinuccio, Barbara's young man; for although she was only eighteen, Barbara was already as good as engaged; he was a steady young man of twenty-six, a law graduate; his family lived in Sicily, they were rather grand and disapproved of the engagement but they were old-fashioned and full of bourgeois prejudices like all the decadent nobility, said Signora Fontana, and were bound to come round in the end.

My mother found Jozek there as usual when she came in, and because it was Saturday I was there too. As always, Jozek was hoping to be asked to stay for dinner, and remembering that Signora Fontana always had guests, my mother curtly invited him. During supper she told us all about her meeting with Signora Fontana; and Jozek, who always liked to give the

82

impression that he knew everybody, naturally said that he knew Signora Fontana: ah yes, short in the legs and long in the tooth, with a red-haired daughter; they had been living near some friends of his last year; the mother was an inveterate busybody, the daughter a young trollop. When Jozek said this, my mother was furious and called him a malicious scandal-monger, a poison-tongued snake; doubtless he had made a pass at the girl and had been put in his place so he was trying to get his own back. Chaim, as always, tried to soothe my mother: they were probably talking about completely different people. But my mother was in a bad temper for the rest of the evening, and decided that this was the last time she would ever invite Jozek to dinner; he had no idea how to behave and had helped himself to three large slices of meat which meant that there was none left for tomorrow.

We spent the whole of that Sunday, my mother and I, sorting out old letters and sticking old photos into an album. Chaim was not the only one to possess a family album, said my mother, we had one too. Giulia stayed in bed feeling unwell. She was pregnant and complained of nausea and giddiness. Chaim had gone to a concert with Jozek, Costanza was playing ball with Carmela in the garden. Soon, said my mother, in a few years' time, Giulia's child would be playing ball in the garden; she could only hope that it would not take too much after Chaim, and much less after Jozek: what a hateful person that Jozek was, she said, with his poisonous tongue, his scandal-mongering. But when she came across some old photos of Giulia and me when we were little, my mother softened; here was Giulia with her long legs, black stockings, a sailor-collar and the big straw hat tied with ribbons under her chin. To think she was now going to have a baby! The thought of Giulia's baby due in the summer touched my mother, but not to the extent of making her forget her usual complaints. She had only heard about the baby that very day and then quite by chance from the recumbent Giulia; and that was the only way, chance, that one could ever get information from Giulia, even about the most important things. And when the baby was born, she said, perhaps Chaim would at last make up his mind to earn some money; it was a disgrace that a man of forty should still have to rely upon his mother-in-law for nearly everything; it was just as well that she had been able to let the house in Dronero and that she had her husband's pension and those few acres of vineyards on the slopes of San Damiano; and she also had a few shares in Italgas. Without this income, heaven knows how they would have managed. No one, she told me, was ever to know about the Italgas shares, that was her secret, because if her sisters got to hear about it they were bound to ask her to repay the money she had borrowed to buy the house here in town. She would pay them back just as soon as she won her case against the Dronero council, who had taken over two properties for the nursery school without paying her anything like the market value. I asked why she did not sell a few of her Italgas shares and set Chaim up in a decent practice; and my mother was very offended and told me that I knew nothing about business matters, that I was an absolute greenhorn and here I was thinking I knew all about it.

But when I was about to leave, my mother made me a peace-offering of a pendant we had found turning out a drawer full of old photos, and she told me that Signora Fontana had invited her to tea the following Tuesday, feeling obliged to my mother for having insisted on paying the whole bill at the coffee-bar; and Barbara had had that big strawberry ice. Signora Fontana had especially asked my mother to bring Giulia and myself along, because my mother had been able to get in a few words eventually and reveal the fact of our existence. She said she didn't believe a word of what that malicious scandalmonger, Jozek, had said; on the contrary, these were thoroughly respectable people as anyone could tell just by looking at them. Afraid that I might refuse, she told me that Signora Fontana knew masses of people and could be very useful in finding pupils for me. I said that I had plenty of pupils and no need of any more, but I promised to go with her.

So on Tuesday afternoon all three of us set out for Via Tripoli, my sister and I walking on either side of my mother;

84

what a long time it was, she said, since the three of us had been out together. She was happy but a little anxious in case we should arrive late. None of us knew the way to Via Tripoli and we found ourselves wandering around an area of newly-built houses and unpaved roads among puddles and patches of grass streaked with dirty snow. When we found Via Tripoli at last, it was hardly more than a ditch bordered by hedges leading to a small courtyard heaped with snow and sheets of metal. On the far side stood a tall, narrow apartment block, reaching up like a tower into the fog and backing on to fields.

Not a very cheerful place, my mother observed as we climbed the stairs, but prices were, of course, exorbitant right in town and even she had had to buy on the outskirts; still, she preferred her own area and wondered how Signora Fontana coped with the mud wearing only sandals; the district was seedy, there was no lift and the stairs were very tiring; she rested on the way up, took a handkerchief from her pocket and wiped the snow off her shoes.

The door was opened by the maid, Settimia, a little old woman bundled up in shawls. She led us down a passage and into a tiny room, sparsely furnished and dimly lit. Through a half-open door on to the passage, we could see a bedroom with the beds still unmade and a nightdress rolled up untidily on the pillow. In a corner of the sitting room, on a divan covered with a Sardinian rug, lay the cat Menelao — a wild-looking Siamese who fled at our approach. We sat around a table that had a small cactus in a pot in the middle, and my mother immediately crossed her fingers because cacti are un-lucky. We sat and waited, watching the light draining from the bleak fields beyond the windows; and my mother observed testily that we need not have hurried so much through all that mud, and how discourteous it was not to be at home to receive us having asked us to come.

Signora Fontana arrived at last, and her daughter with her. She was laden with parcels and apologized for having kept us waiting, explaining that she had had things to do all over town: Barbara was going to a rather special ball in a few days.

She undid the packages and showed us the tulle and velvet she had bought. She had designed the dress herself: it was to have a tight bodice and a full skirt with three soft pleats at the back and three in front and a spray of rosebuds at the neck; a floating, filmy creation, very *jeune fille*. My mother listened unsmilingly, still offended about having had to wait. Silk roses or fresh, she asked brusquely. Fresh roses, naturally, replied Signora Fontana. Then Settimia appeared with the tea; and to go with the tea we were offered some big, rock-hard biscuits of a kind usually found only in milk-bars.

My mother asked to see the paintings and Signora Fontana led us into another room with piles of canvases stacked against the walls. We looked at livid, elongated heads of indeterminate sex with little crosses for eyes and metal grills for mouths, set against backgrounds of rows and rows of houses and cross-hatched skies, rows of houses with barred windows and crooked chimneys that emitted a livid smoke.

Ah yes, said my mother, this was modern art. So many people failed to understand it, but she understood it; her only criticism was that these paintings seemed rather sad, they reminded her of a prison; but the bar motif was probably due to the influence of this area, which was maybe a little gloomy and reminiscent of a prison with all those high buildings that suggested prisons and barracks and was surrounded by such a desolate tract of open land. But Signora Fontana disagreed with my mother about the area which, she said, was really not gloomy at all; we should see it in the spring when the grass was covered with wild anemones; she would wake up in the morning to the tinkle of sheep-bells, and would take her palette and brushes and paint outside sitting on the grass.

After studying Giulia intently for a few moments, Signora Fontana remarked that she had a beautiful and interesting head; she would love to paint it, and what a pity that the light was no longer good enough. This pleased my mother greatly and she told Signora Fontana proudly about Giulia's expecting a baby. Signora Fontana said that when the baby was born, Giulia should come to her for advice as she had once worked in a children's home, at a time when she badly needed money. She had had some very difficult times in her life, she said, and had always managed to come through them without being beholden to anybody. Her husband Gilberto, bless him, was not the dependable type: he had a weak character, very easily influenced. Their marriage had not even lasted a whole year, but they had remained good friends. As a girl she had studied ballet and had been spoiled and over-protected by her family; then financial disaster and the break-up of the family; and to support herself she had done a bit of everything, relying solely on her own resources. She had been a member of an amateur theatrical company; she had worked in journalism; she had been secretary to a politician and as he was a widower she had also run his household and acted as hostess at his dinners and official receptions where she had sat next to ambassadors and ministers of state. She had rubbed shoulders with all sorts and conditions of people; her whole life had been like the pages of a novel and maybe, before she died, she would write her memoirs.

My mother told her that I had a great gift for writing: I had written little poems as a child and my essays had been read by the whole school; I was extremely gifted and now worked in the editorial department of a magazine; what with coaching private pupils, working on the magazine and studying late at night for my degree, her great fear was that I might be driving myself into nervous exhaustion. She asked Signora Fontana what she thought of my appearance; what did she think should be done about my hair. Signora Fontana took my head between her hands and twisted it this way and that, pondering and wrinkling her nose; at last she said that her advice would be to have it cut very short and permed very, very lightly. Then she told her daughter to take us girls into the other room, and after all, Giulia with her fresh young face was still a girl too, and show us her clothes and all her other little things, while she and my mother had a chat about the art gallery.

Following the pony-tail as it swung, flaming, over a black school overall, we went to the bedroom which had, in the meantime, been hastily tidied with the beds made and covered over; we sat on the beds and Barbara laughed and admitted that she had nothing special in the way of clothes to show us. Her mother, she said, was always bluffing about everything; she had two nice dresses but they were nothing out of the ordinary; perhaps the gown her mother was making for the ball would be quite nice. The ball was important because some of her fiancé's relatives from Sicily were here on holiday and they would be there, and he was going to introduce her to them, hoping that they would take a liking to her and speak in favour of the marriage when they returned to Sicily; none of Pinuccio's family had ever wanted to see even a photograph of her, because they were absolutely set against his marrying any girl outside his own region; they were very strange, very haughty people, minor nobility with pots of money, and they lived shut away in a castle on a cliff-top from where one could see nothing at all except prickly pears and the sea. Pinuccio's father weighed over a hundred kilograms and could only get up the stairs by leaning on the shoulders of two servants; and there were several sisters, old maids, who still wore mourning for an uncle who had died in the war and because of that could never leave the castle grounds; they baked their own bread, knitted strange black stockings as long as snakes and recited the rosary every evening around the lamp. If she married Pinuccio, this was the kind of life she would be expected to lead, and she found the prospect very uninviting. She was trying to persuade Pinuccio to settle in the north. In a few months he would be qualified and there was nothing to stop him practising in Rome or Turin. Yet he seemed determined to return to Sicily and only dreamed of the day when he would lead her up the steps through the rocks to the castle and they would go into a shadowy room as big as a parade ground and kiss the hand of that father of his who weighed over a hundred kilos.

Pinuccio refused to eat ordinary bread bought from shops, and his sisters sent him these round loaves with hard crusts that crumbled as soon as you tried to slice them because, of course, they were stale; and they sent him salamis covered with peppercorns and a kind of sweet made from honey and egg-white; she had once tasted one of these sweets and for the rest of the day her mouth felt as though she'd been chewing a bar of soap. Whenever he came to dinner, Pinuccio always criticized the food because he only liked Sicilian cooking; and he was critical about her clothes and the way she walked, and heaven help her if she wiggled her behind the teeniest bit; and if he caught her wearing lipstick, he was quite capable of smacking her face. He was terribly jealous, and he was conditioned by his sisters' way of life: they never went out alone and never bathed in the sea even though it was on the doorstep; they didn't even possess swimming costumes. She had a costume, a very decent all-in-one just slightly cut away at the back, but whenever she and Pinuccio went to the swimming-pool together, there was an argument about her costume. And if he ever saw her laughing and joking with another boy, he was like an enraged tiger.

Pinuccio made her life very difficult, yet she loved him and put up with everything without a fuss because of her love. At night she would often lie awake for hours trying to compose a letter to tell Pinuccio that she never wanted to see him again. Her mother would turn on the light and see her there with her eyes wide open, and would be anxious and get up to make some camomile tea and tell her to forget all about Pinuccio or she would make herself ill. Yet her mother was also very fond of Pinuccio and was always saying that men like him, hard-working, affectionate, rich and handsome, were few and far between; and a husband's looks were important, her mother said. They would stay awake chatting all night, she and her mother, and eating the liqueur chocolates that Pinuccio gave her; and finally her mother would try to comfort her, saying that Pinuccio would probably change in time and be more tolerant, and perhaps he would agree not to return to Sicily.

She would run off to school without even time for a cup of coffee and in class would be too tired to attend properly after a sleepless night, and when questioned on her homework would get only four out of ten because she was too sleepy to think. She told herself that this was not important, because she was about to be married and drop her studies anyway, but she was ashamed of herself all the same and would come out of school in tears; but Pinuccio was always waiting for her, looking so handsome in his camel overcoat, and he comforted her and took her to the park; and she gradually forgot all about the low marks and the gloomy prospect of life in Sicily. When Pinuccio was in a good mood, he seemed a different person from the man who had, on some occasions, grabbed hold of the lapels of her coat, his face as white as a sheet, just because some idiot boy had waved to her.

As she spoke, Barbara played with her pony-tail, pulling it forward on to her chest and combing it with her fingers; and every now and then she turned to look at herself in the dressing-table mirror, fingering the spots on her chin which were the result of eating all those liqueur chocolates; unfortunately, she said, all these nice things harmed one in some way, and with the ball only a few days away she would have to stop eating liqueur chocolates if she was to appear with a clear skin. She told Giulia that she envied her lovely complexion; how did she manage to keep her skin so smooth? Her red hair, she said, complemented Giulia's skin perfectly; and sitting close to Giulia, she slid an arm round Giulia's waist and held her pony-tail next to Giulia's face and they looked at themselves together in the glass. But she was fed up with her red mop, she said: her class-mates called her Goldilocks.

When we went back to the sitting room, my mother and Signora Fontana were already on first-name terms. They had certainly had a good talk ranging over a multitude of subjects and had decided that the art gallery as projected by my mother should become a joint venture for the two of them; and it was going to be wonderful and exciting, a true intellectual centre in a city which had, up to now, catered so inadequately for the arts. They were sitting together on the divan like old friends, with an ashtray brimful of cigarette butts and mandarin peel beside them. Menelao was sitting on my mother's knee, and as soon as we appeared she said that cats were better than dogs and Giulia's puppy had tried her patience to the limit. Seeing the three of us enter together, Signora Fontana cried that she simply had to do a group portrait of us. My mother, agreeing, said that I should have to be decently dressed, however: she couldn't bear that dreadful sweater, it made me look like a Russian factory-worker. But Signora Fontana, or Scilla as my mother now called her, said she liked the sweater, and when we posed for the portrait Barbara too would wear a sweater; and she wanted us to sit on the divan, in the corner by the window, with a dish of mandarins on one side and Menelao on the other. We must come tomorrow without fail to pose for her. I murmured that I wouldn't have time, that I had to study; but as my mother pushed me towards the door she declared that I could certainly spare an hour to pose for my portrait. We were held up for a few minutes at the door because my mother had asked Scilla to lend her some novels and Scilla was looking through a small bookcase; she pulled out a few volumes, old books, she said, that belonged to her husband, because she only read very seldom; she loved reading but had to save her eyesight for painting; sometimes her daughter read to her aloud. Scilla and Barbara stood with their arms around each other, exchanging playful kisses and little endearments: 'frou-frou', 'bijou'; but then Settimia the maid screeched out that the food was ready. Settimia the maid always called her mistress 'Scilla' and used the familiar 'tu' when she spoke to her. Scilla whispered to my mother that there was no way she could persuade Settimia to be more formal and polite, but it didn't really matter because Settimia had nursed her as a baby and had been with the family for years. We were already late, so my mother tucked the books that Scilla had lent her under her arm without even looking at them and we went downstairs quickly. On our way out of the courtyard we passed a pale young man with long black hair, Pinuccio without a doubt, because we knew that he was expected.

In the tram on the way home, my mother picked Menelao's

hairs off her skirt; then she glanced at the titles of the books she had borrowed and was taken slightly aback to find she had been lent *The Three Musketeers*: children's books, books suitable for young Costanza. Scilla must have made a mistake; she had asked her for some good modern novels; Scilla's sight was probably very weak, and that would explain why she painted in that way, with all those bars and railings. Doubtless, in the portrait she was going to do tomorrow, we two girls, Barbara, the cat and the mandarins would all be reduced to a series of bars and railings.

I was sitting opposite Giulia in the tram and noticed that her cheeks had some colour in them and that her timid smile was happier than usual; my mother noticed this too and pointed out to Chaim as soon as we got home how well Giulia looked this evening, all because she had agreed to go out and enjoy a little company; it was very important, she said, to spend some time with other people, otherwise one became bored, and boredom was bad for the liver. She gave Chaim a detailed account of our afternoon, such a nice afternoon and such pleasant people; and she told him about Scilla's having done so many different things and having rubbed shoulders with all kinds of people and having even worked for a time in a children's home. But Chaim seemed unhappy that Giulia was planning to go again the next day because it was a long way to go and he feared she would get tired; posing, too, was always tiring. This made my mother cross and she told Chaim that he didn't know what he was talking about, that he was useless as a doctor; and she curled up on the sofa, put on her glasses and began to read *The Three Musketeers* because she had never read it and had nothing better to read.

The next day, Giulia was unwell and stayed in bed all day, so my mother and I went to Scilla's without her. My mother was most annoyed about Giulia's staying at home and said that she was sure there was nothing wrong with her and that Chaim must have refused to let her come out; she was perfectly well apart from a touch of nerves; since her marriage Giulia had become more dull and dispirited than ever; once she had at least cared a little about her clothes and read the occasional fashion magazine, but now she seemed to have lost interest even in that. Perhaps the arrival of the baby would liven her up a bit. Did Chaim and Giulia get on together? Who could tell. They never quarrelled, at least never in public; but if Chaim attempted to stroke Giulia's hair, as he did sometimes, Giulia would jerk her head away and the doctor's hand would fly convulsively to his tie and his shoulder would twitch violently. Sometimes, on a Sunday, he sat beside her and offered to read Hofmannsthal's poetry to her as he used to do; but Giulia would request him not to read to her because she had no desire to listen, and ask him to sit further away because the smell of his cigarette was unpleasant to her. My mother said that it would have been different if Giulia had married a different sort of man, someone younger and jollier; Chaim was a man who no longer believed in anything, he had been through too much. Once he had been a Communist, when he was younger; now he had given up being a Communist, he was nothing at all; my mother hated the Communists, yet it would almost have been better if Chaim had stayed a Communist; and she often remonstrated with Chaim, saying that at least the Communists had some vision of the future, but what vision did he have, nothing at all. He did not even believe in his profession; it was all the same to him whether a patient lived or died, since, according to him, life had nothing to offer anyway; of course, with this sort of attitude he could hardly expect to attract many patients: he exuded cynicism and bitterness from every pore. She was sure that his own patients had no respect for him; and he went round with that timid little smile, so sour and dejected-looking, that showed his broken teeth smashed by a punch in the face during an anti-Semitic demonstration in Poland many years ago.

Scilla began the portrait of Barbara and me together as soon as we arrived. Barbara had put on a bright green ski-sweater with a high polo-neck. We arranged ourselves on the divan with the cat, but the cat jumped down and ran off; and there was no dish of mandarin oranges because Barbara had eaten them all at lunch-time and Settimia had refused point-blank to go out and buy more. Scilla had donned a kind of smock, long and much smeared with paint, and as she worked she grumbled about Settimia to my mother, saying that she was as slow as a snail and it took hours to persuade her to pop down a couple of flights of stairs; she would dearly like to engage a younger maid. But my mother told her to beware of young housemaids, look at our Carmela, for instance, who was always breaking things.

In no time at all the picture was done. It was just as my mother had predicted: livid, elongated heads, one topped by a frizz of hair, the other by a fiery plume, crosses for eyes and railings for mouths. But Scilla was very happy with it; she had captured, she said, the very essence of modern life: these were today's young women, fearless, uninhibited, without frill or affectation, built to fight beside their menfolk; and she stuck a label on it saying *Girls in Sweaters* — its official title for the catalogue of the coming exhibition at my mother's gallery, which would be her first one-man show. My mother merely commented that Scilla had not really done justice to my eyes; my lively, expressive eyes, she said, were my only good feature, take them away and I was left with nothing. As I got ready to go, Scilla's ex-husband Gilberto arrived: a youngish man but already quite bald, with a drooping Mexican moustache and a raincoat frayed at the cuffs. He sat down with his coat on, complaining that the flat was like a fridge and telling Settimia to bring him a cognac. Settimia called Gilberto, too, by his first name and was very short with him. If the flat was cold why did he bother to come, she wanted to know; but she poured him out a glass of cognac and offered some to us as well. We declined and she bore the bottle away with her at once: this one, she said, was quite capable of draining the bottle if one didn't look out. She continued to shout oaths and insults from the kitchen, much to my mother's embarrassment, but Scilla said to take no notice, poor old Settimia

94

hardly knew what she was doing any more and often talked to herself. Gilberto heaved a cushion in the direction of the kitchen. He asked Scilla why on earth she didn't get rid of the peppery old bat, and Scilla replied that the peppery old bat had nursed her as a child. Gilberto turned his attention to the portrait, stroking his moustache as he looked at it and finally making a non-committal gurgling noise at the back of his throat. Barbara leant over the back of his chair whispering 'Daddykins, Daddykins' over and over again, and now and then he reached up a hand decked with an amethyst ring and tugged her pony-tail.

I went off and left my mother there; she tried to persuade me to stay longer but it was already late and I had to hurry to reach the other side of town in time for a lesson. But throughout the lesson, a Latin coaching session with a lazy, unmotivated child, I continued to think about these people my mother had got in with; and I felt slightly uneasy, as if vaguely sensing something suspicious beneath the surface, but try as I might, I was unable to define or clarify the feeling.

Reaching home, I found my friend preparing a little supper for us. We ate it by the window, leaning on the sill and looking down at the little square below where people were going in and out of the *osteria* or standing in groups around the street-lamps, stamping their feet with the cold while others played with the water jetting from the little fountain on the corner. We were very fond of this little square, its fountain, its lamps and neon signs and the bronze statue that stood in the middle, its base now hidden under the snow. For me, the square and our tiny kitchen and the room with its books and the table I used for studying were a haven of refuge, to which I could always return for peace and comfort. In a few months' time, my friend would be married and I should be left alone in that room, spending every evening alone jotting down notes with a red pencil in the margins of magazines about all the things I had to remember. I should be very lonely and sad without the austere presence of my friend sitting beside me, smoking and reading and flicking the ash from the pages with her large, dear, capable hand. My friend was a great support, and it distressed me to think that I should be deprived in great measure of this support when she married, for then I would see much less of her. I told her what I was thinking, and she laughed and put her warm, firm hand over mine and said that, on the contrary, she intended to come and see me very often and take me back to dinner in her flat, where there was going to be a splendid machine for making milk-shakes. We had always enjoyed these shakes made with all kinds of fruit; some relatives were giving her the machine for a wedding present, and it was truly magnificent, just like the ones they had in bars. So the milk-shake equipment put an end to our previous discussion, and this was typical of my friend who hated sad, self-indulgent topics and always diverted them towards something solid and concrete. I knew this trait well; and I was happy to be distracted, borne away, as it were, in the palm of her imperious hand, whenever I found myself becoming maudlin. Besides, said my friend when we were getting ready for bed, it was time I thought about getting married myself. I said that of course I should like to get married, but somehow I felt that it would never happen to me. I mustn't give way to such negative thoughts, she said: they were woolly and senseless and only cluttered the mind like unhealthy vapours.

I learnt later that my mother had had to bring the portrait away with her that same evening. Scilla had made her a present of it and had absolutely insisted that she carry it away with her at once. She had framed it and wrapped it and stuffed it under my mother's arm; and my mother had had a dreadful struggle to hump it as far as the tram-stop. So the *Girls in Sweaters* now looked out from the dining-room wall, gazing over Chaim's shoulder with their eyes like little crosses.

Our visits to Signora Fontana and her daughter now became a matter of course; and even Carmela was obliged to visit old Settimia sometimes on a Sunday afternoon, when she never knew what to do with herself and tended to stand the whole time by the kitchen window, gloomily rubbing her elbows and pulling at the sleeves of her cardigan. My mother hoped that Settimia would teach Carmela some good recipes. So Carmela was pressed into accompanying my mother to Via Tripoli, and she and Settimia trudged together along the lanes and footpaths between the fields. But she came back looking even more vacant and sullen than usual after trudging along the footpaths. She hated the whole district and said that it was even uglier and emptier than her old house in Dronero, there was nothing but fields; and Settimia knew nothing about cooking. Settimia, she said, had told her that she wasn't really a housemaid at all, but a close relative of Signora Fontana's who had fallen upon hard times; and Signora Fontana passed her off as the maid because otherwise people would know that she had no servant. My mother replied that Settimia was mad and one couldn't believe a word she said; whereupon Carmela wanted to know why, then, was she sent to spend her Sunday with someone who was mad; if she had to be with mad people, she might as well stay with her own father. And Settimia walked so slowly that they had both got cold trudging around the footpaths in that God-forsaken place; and Settimia dressed most peculiarly, with a little cape with pearls sewn all over it; she looked like an old witch and the boys threw snowballs at her. Still, she didn't think that Settimia was really mad, a bit strange, perhaps, but hardly mad. As things turned out, Carmela was not required to spend many Sunday afternoons with Settimia, because before long Settimia vanished from the Fontana household. Scilla told my mother that she had sent her back to her village with a handsome sum of money because she had got too old and too mad to do anything properly. Scilla now looked after the flat herself, wearing rubber gloves to protect her hands; and she said that it amused her to keep busy about the place and to mess about in the kitchen experimenting with interesting recipes. She had decided not to engage another housemaid for the moment; housemaids were all the same, irritating and spendthrift; later, maybe, she would employ a manservant, because some friends had told her that men worked harder than women around the house. My mother asked whether she and Barbara would feel safe at night alone in the house with a manservant; but Scilla said that her friends would recommend someone completely trustworthy, they had suggested a relative of their own chauffeur; certainly they would not want her to engage a complete stranger. But my mother was against the whole idea; even with the highest credentials, a man is always a man and might suddenly get funny ideas. And then Scilla had no conception of how much food a man could get through; while a woman might be satisfied by a light meal, a man's appetite was quite another story. My mother told Scilla that her friends had put a harebrained scheme into her head, while she could easily have written to cousin Teresa in Dronero, asking her to send her some nice country girl. My mother was slightly jealous of these friends of Scilla's about whom she heard so much, and was secretly hoping that Scilla would introduce her to them sooner or later; they were wealthy people who had a car and often invited Scilla to spend a few days with them at their country estate a few miles out of town. Every time she went, Scilla returned with an upset stomach from eating too much and had to go on a strict diet consisting mainly of boiled chicory and stewed-fruit purée.

When Scilla was away staying with her friends, my mother hardly knew what to do with herself; she had got into the habit of spending every afternoon with Scilla, and when her friend was away she would sit in the coffee-bar sipping her granita with whipped cream and puzzling her brain about why Scilla was always promising to introduce her to these friends yet never actually arranging to do so; and she wondered if Scilla was not, perhaps, rather vague and indecisive; for example, she would talk for hours about the art gallery, promising to bring along all her friends and acquaintances and suggesting that she and my mother should take it in turns to give little talks about a wide variety of subjects, even, perhaps, about the emancipation of women, but although she and my mother had been to see dozens of possible places, she never approved of any of them. As far as the rent for such places was concerned, Scilla had told my mother not to worry: her friends had so much money that they would, she was sure, advance them all they needed. But surely, my mother mused, the first thing that Scilla should have done was to introduce her to these friends.

On days like this, out of sheer desperation my mother would end up going to her sisters' shop; she nosed around the merchandise, sat down for a cigarette in the stock-room and told the delivery man to send her round some used packing cases and a little straw which would be useful to Carmela for lighting the boiler; and her sisters, much more kindly disposed to her now that they saw her less often, gave her some rolls of twine for hanging out the washing and, producing a bottle of egg marsala, offered her half a glass. My mother grumbled about their not even having a biscuit, saying that drinking marsala on an empty stomach made her head spin.

Entering Scilla's flat one day, my mother noticed an umbrella lying on the sofa, one of the telescopic kind that close up small enough to fit into a handbag. Scilla told her that it belonged to Valeria, one of the country-house set; she had left only a moment ago and had forgotten to take her umbrella. My mother smelt perfume in the air: it was *coeur de lilas*, said Scilla; Valeria had left only ten minutes ago; my mother had probably passed her in the street; had she not noticed a tall, fine-looking woman in a beaver coat? No, said my mother, no one like that had passed her; and as for the beaver coat, if she had the means, beaver would be the last fur she would choose: one saw it everywhere nowadays. But Valeria, Scilla explained, only wore her beaver coat when it rained: it was like a raincoat. She wanted to show my mother how pretty the umbrella was, and opened it up; but my mother told her to put it down immediately, because opening an umbrella indoors was unlucky.

Scilla kept saying what a shame it was that my mother had not arrived earlier; she wanted her to meet Valeria and was curious to know what she would think of her. She had strong features, she said, an unusual face with a determined jaw and aquiline nose; and she pushed her own jaw forward to demonstrate what Valeria's was like. And my mother, who was sitting on the divan rolling up the umbrella, observed that if Scilla had been so keen on her meeting Valeria, all she had needed to do was to telephone and ask her to come a little earlier; for my mother had installed a phone some time previously, being obliged to do so for Chaim. Scilla replied that it hadn't occurred to her to telephone; she had no phone herself so it would have meant going downstairs to the bakery; she had avoided having a phone in the flat because with the number of friends she had it would have been ringing all day and she would never get a moment's peace. But my mother said that she failed to understand why she had never met a single one of all these friends, including Valeria, that Scilla claimed to possess. It was so strange, this, as to be almost incredible. And where were all these fine friends? She and Scilla were constantly out together, going to coffee-bars and cinemas, yet never, ever, had Scilla been greeted by anyone. Scilla replied that her friends hardly ever walked around the town; they all had their cars and only went to the very best establishments where a cup of chocolate was capable of costing five hundred lire, never to the humble coffee-bars that she and my mother went to. My mother retorted that she had no complaints about the 'humble coffee-bars' they went to, and she couldn't afford to throw money about especially when she was nearly always the one who had to pay because Scilla either left her purse at home or disappeared into the cloakroom just at the moment when the bill came. My mother suddenly felt herself flushing with anger and sweating under the armpits; red patches appeared on her neck and she began to rattle her pearls furiously against her chest; snatching up her fur coat, she swept out. But she had barely got two floors down when Scilla came running after her; kissing her on both cheeks, she took her back to the flat, settled her once more on the divan and begged her not to leave her alone because she was upset and had so many problems on her mind.

My mother sat and listened to Scilla's problems for some

considerable time. Scilla had very little money; she had invested her small capital in a few shares, but because she was constantly having to draw out money for living expenses, the capital was dwindling rapidly; she had her work of course, designing clothes for couturiers, but such work was not highly paid and there were times when the demand tailed off completely; at the moment, in fact, she had nothing on hand at all. Besides, she had an awkward character and sometimes struck people as being supercilious and overbearing; there were some employers who refused to use her again because she had once answered back when provoked by a silly remark. The solution would be to work for herself; her dream was to set up her own little dressmaking business, or, better still, not a dressmaker's but one of those little dress shops which make clothes to measure and also sell elegant accessories like shoes and watches, slacks, gloves and scarves. She would take endless pleasure in creating her own originals, designing clothes with flair, with that something extra; it would be a success, she was sure of it; she had been talking about it only that afternoon to Valeria, and she had asked her for a loan, at least to get started; although she had a little capital of her own, she preferred not to have to touch it. Valeria had promised to lend her the money, but she would have to ask her husband's permission first, and he was a difficult sort of person and very tight-fisted; he was so mean, in fact, that when the maid put away the winter clothes, he insisted that his wife count the mothballs. So there was no knowing if he would agree to the loan, and Scilla had a feeling he might refuse. This was why she hadn't mentioned the art gallery to Valeria, she said, because it was best to tackle one thing at a time. The art gallery was a wonderful idea, of course, the only pity was that it would not be very profitable; and she needed to earn some money quickly; and she needed, too, to find an outlet for her energy in something positive, some project that would give her immediate satisfaction. The art gallery was more of a long-term project, would take time to organize and be full of risk and uncertainty; besides, she was not feeling very close to art at the moment and was

101

itching to get to grips with something that would show immediate, tangible results on a more mundane level; she was not enjoying her painting at the moment, finding that as soon as she had prepared her palette and brushes and put in a few strokes, her neck would start to ache and her eyes water; perhaps she was suffering from slight nervous exhaustion. But she was full of plans and projects for the little dress shop. In a little while, no doubt, she would return to her painting with renewed energy, before long, when Barbara was married and she had less on her mind. At the moment, apart from everything else, the wedding was getting closer and she had to think about the trousseau: she could hardly send her off to that castle in Sicily with nothing, to all those spinster sisters who hated her even before they had ever set eyes on her; she must have a decent trousseau, or they would say that Pinuccio had married a pauper. Gilberto, bless him, had offered to sell his amethyst ring, even though it meant so much to him that he wore it night and day; but Gilberto had no idea about the expense of a trousseau and had never realized that his ring was actually worth very little. Gilberto, unfortunately, had his own problems at the moment; the business was doing badly and although he was obliged by law to pay her a certain sum every month, he had been going through such a bad patch lately that he hadn't actually been able to send her anything and she hadn't had the heart to insist; Gilberto wasn't a fit man, he had a gastric ulcer and had to avoid stress.

My mother said that as far as the shop was concerned, she would have no objection to becoming involved, even to becoming a partner. She would not concern herself with the design and tailoring side, because she had no experience in that field, even though she had often given her cousins and nieces in Dronero the benefit of her advice, consulting the fashion magazines and especially *Vogue*. But she could certainly keep the books and deal with customers: here she would be in her element, and besides she had done this already in her sisters' china shop; it was just unfortunate that her sisters' ideas were so limited and she did not see eye to eye with them.

In a voice that was husky with emotion, she told Scilla that she had a few Italgas shares in the bank and would willingly raise some capital to help her set up the shop. To tell the truth, she had already promised this money to Chaim, her son-in-law Dr Wesser; but she had a right to put her own interests first, because after all, Chaim could manage very well for a time to visit his patients using his scooter; she had no great faith in Chaim's future; it was certainly not the lack of his own practice that was holding him back. She intended to put her own interests first; she, like Scilla, was full of energy and was not yet ready to sit at home mending socks and looking after grandchildren; later on, when the shop was earning money, she could do something about Chaim's practice. Scilla nodded gravely, frowning and running her fingers through her straw-coloured shock of hair; then she went to fetch the bottle of cognac and they toasted the success of their enterprise.

They agreed that within the next few days, as soon as Valeria's husband had made a decision, the three of them, Valeria, Scilla and my mother, would meet and begin to formulate a concrete plan for the realization of their objective. But, Scilla insisted, they must not lose sight of the art gallery, so they should choose spacious and well-lit premises that could, at a later date, be transformed into a gallery; the dress shop would be only a kind of temporary measure to produce immediate cash in hand and also bring them to the notice of the public. What name should they choose for the shop? They both racked their brains; Scilla favoured something French: *coup de foudre*, *fanfan la tulipe*, *rayon de bonheur*, but my mother disapproved; when it came to shops with French names, she said, there were already enough and to spare for the parish poor. They turned to the signs of the Zodiac: Aries, Libra, Capricorn. My mother's birth-sign was Aries, and she had no objection at all to the name of Aries; Scilla's sign was Sagittarius. That was the one to choose, Scilla cried: they would never find a more apt or more beautiful name than Sagittarius. And it was perfectly suitable for an art gallery too, so come the day when scarves and gloves gave way to paintings, they would

103

not even have to change the name.

Now that this was settled, Scilla returned to the subject of her problems. Barbara was a great source of anxiety; her fiancé was so jealous and she was constantly worried that they would quarrel and break it off. Barbara took after her mother in every way, she was all sunshine and showers, a prickly personality. Her fiancé's jealousy only spurred her on to flirt with her classmates on purpose to tease him. She meant no harm by it, it was only girlish high spirits, but he was always threatening to fight duels with one or another of them and commit mayhem. Take the night of the ball, for instance. Scilla had been up for two nights running, cutting out and making up the dress, and it had turned out beautifully: Barbara had looked divine in all that tulle, with the fresh rosebuds and her hair flowing loose. Scilla hadn't looked bad either, in her old lamé gown. Pinuccio's relatives had been there, a married couple from Sicily, the wife all tricked out in purple like a bishop, the husband wearing a dinner-jacket that was too tight for him, his neck brown and wrinkled like a peasant's and great tufts of hair sprouting from his nose and ears. They looked as if they had crawled out from some cave in Catania: third-rate people with narrow, provincial minds. Well, Pinuccio had taken Scilla and Barbara over to them and had made the introductions; and they had merely shaken their hands limply and then turned away. Barbara was naturally very upset; she blushed to the roots of her hair and didn't know where to look; and Pinuccio was dreadfully embarrassed, and stood between Barbara and his relatives, screwing his handkerchief into a ball and shifting from one foot to the other; eventually Barbara turned her back on him, gathered her skirts about her and marched off alone. She was immediately surrounded by a crowd of young men, dancing, laughing, drinking champagne and making far too much noise; and Pinuccio's relatives were looking more glum with every minute that passed, and Pinuccio just stood by the curtains, chain-smoking and pulling bits out of the curtain with hands that sweated. Scilla had gone up to him to ask why he didn't join in the dancing, and he had been extremely rude to her; the memory of his words made Scilla want to cry. They had come away from the ball alone because when it was time to go they couldn't find Pinuccio; and Scilla had decided against calling a taxi because of the expense; but Marchese Petrocchi noticed them walking away and drove after them and insisted on giving them a lift home. The Marchese had been dancing with Barbara all evening and was wearing one of her roses in his buttonhole. When they got home, Pinuccio was waiting outside, huddled on the back seat of a taxi. Heaven knows how long he had been sitting there and the meter running all this time. Anyway, Pinuccio leapt from the taxi and confronted the Marchese, wrenching the rose out of his buttonhole; he was on the verge of punching the Marchese, and Scilla and Barbara were screaming, but luckily the Marchese was a man with his wits about him and he turned the whole thing into a joke, then Scilla invited both men up to the flat to sort out the quarrel; she gave them each a cognac and Pinuccio gradually calmed down and eventually apologized to them and to the Marchese; in the end, the two men went off together in a very friendly way and the Marchese was even offering to lend Pinuccio his car the next day so that he could take his relations out for a drive. She and Barbara, however, had been left exhausted and with their nerves in shreds; and she had scolded Barbara for behaving so badly at the ball; there were times when her shouts and laughter must have been heard quite clearly outside in the street. Then Barbara had got so cross that she had torn her dress as she was taking it off.

Honestly, said Scilla, it was no easy matter bringing up a daughter; and one might think that in this day and age certain prejudices would have disappeared; but not a bit of it; in fact, she had found that because she was separated from her husband she was fair game for all the evil gossip; and Barbara, just because she was a bit boisterous and high-spirited, was accused of being a flirt when she was really only a bit of a monkey. My mother said that Barbara's reputation was not in fact very good, and that she would be well advised to marry soon because people were saying some very unpleasant things about her. This made Scilla furious and she wanted to know who was spreading evil gossip about her daughter. My mother told her what she had heard from Jozek, Chaim's younger brother; and Scilla wanted to know where this Jozek lived and wanted my mother to take her there straight away so that she could take a stick to him and force him to repeat his filthy accusations to her face. But who was this Jozek anyway? They had never seen him in their lives and wouldn't know him from Adam. What made her really sad, however, was to know that my mother, on hearing such stories, had remained silent and not thrown him out on his ear, the snake. If anyone dared say a word against our family in Scilla's presence, she would react like a tiger. But then she was a true friend and had believed that my mother was her true friend too.

My mother now felt mortified, and told Scilla that although she had not actually thrown Jozek out, she had certainly given him a piece of her mind. And she assured Scilla that of course she could count on her as a true friend; were they not going to be fellow-workers, toiling side by side in perfect amity like a pair of sisters? And there was no need for Scilla to worry excessively about Barbara: attractive and outgoing as she was, even if by any chance she didn't marry Pinuccio she would be bound to have dozens of offers: even the Marchese was paying court to her. But Scilla retorted that the Marchese was married already with four children.

When my mother arrived home that evening, she found that Barbara had come to visit Giulia; the two of them were sitting in the dining-room chatting. Barbara was smoking, but the smoke was apparently not worrying Giulia at all, although she invariably complained of the smell of Chaim's cigarettes. Giulia was looking animated and happy; they had had tea together and had stuffed themselves with liqueur chocolates; Barbara now had the puppy on her knee and was feeding it with the sugar-lumps. My mother was about to tell Barbara not to waste sugar on the dog and that she thought it wrong for an eighteen year old to smoke so much, but in the

106

end she said nothing because she was so pleased to see Giulia looking happy; and she turned on Costanza instead, for spilling a bottle of ink over the table-cloth. She hurried off to put the cloth in to soak, deciding as she did so to write to cousin Teresa asking her to take her daughter away: Costanza was getting nowhere at school and her last report had been dreadful.

Chaim came in with Jozek, Jozek was introduced to Barbara and he immediately began to talk to her about their mutual friends; Barbara could hardly remember these people; ah yes, those neighbours of theirs in Via Lucrezio where they were living a year ago; she and her mother had moved house so often she got confused. Then, in his usual big-headed way, Jozek began to discuss a certain book with her, a novel called *Twilight of the Gods*, doubtless by some long-dead Polish author. Eventually Jozek offered to take Barbara home on the cross-bar of his bicycle, and my mother watched from the window as they climbed on to Jozek's old bone-shaker, Barbara wrapping a scarf tightly round her head to protect it from the wind. There you are, said my mother, that's typical of Jozek: first he spits in the soup, then he eats it.

My mother waited impatiently for Scilla's call throughout the next few days. Scilla had gone off on one of her usual jaunts to Valeria's country estate, leaving Barbara with a school-friend. She never took Barbara with her on these visits because Valeria had no patience with young girls; actually, Valeria had a lover, and had probably no wish to provoke comparisons between her old, wrinkled face and Barbara's young, fresh one. Barbara and Valeria hardly knew each other, anyway, and Scilla was against their meeting because Valeria's language was always rather coarse, rather too free and easy. The arrangement was, therefore, that Scilla would telephone my mother as soon as she returned and fix a time for them all to meet to discuss *Sagittarius*. My mother had said nothing about *Sagittarius* to any of us, planning to do so only when it was well under way; and even then she had no intention of admitting her financial involvement, fearing Giulia and Chaim's reproofs. But feeling guilty about committing money that she had promised Chaim to a completely different enterprise, she made a special effort to be kind to Chaim, asking after his patients and asking his advice about a tonic for Costanza to help her concentrate more at school. My mother was in a very good mood, and she began to prepare for the meeting with the famous Valeria; she tried on different dresses and then selected first a velvet flower and then a paste brooch to adorn the neckline; and sitting in front of the mirror in her bedroom, her chin in her hands and her legs crossed, she admired the sheen of the stocking over her calf; and she rehearsed all the things she was going to say to Valeria, smiling, nodding and knitting her brows; and every now and then she thrust her jaw forward to imitate Valeria's determined sneer or imperious scowl. And one day Costanza came in to tell her that dinner was ready and was stopped in her tracks by the sight of my mother pulling such faces in the mirror. My mother scolded Costanza for entering her room without knocking and, as she went downstairs, complained bitterly about cousin Teresa's failure to bring her children up properly and allowing them to grow up like ragamuffins.

The telephone call from Scilla came at last, one afternoon: they were to meet Valeria at five o'clock in the coffee-bar. My mother was amazed that she should have selected the coffee-bar where they always went instead of one of the smart ones, surely so much more suitable for Valeria, where they charged five hundred lire for a cup of chocolate.

My mother had a long wait in the coffee-bar, sitting there alone, twisting and turning the paste brooch and powdering her nose every five minutes. The day was windy, and the effect of the wind and possibly her own agitated state of mind, had been to make my mother's skin rough and blotchy, and now, after repeated applications of powder, her nose turned yellow. She regretted that Valeria was not going to see her in one of her better moments; the wind had messed up her hair and she tried in vain to poke it back underneath her beret;

she kept opening and closing her bag, dabbed the tip of her nose with her handkerchief and, as always happened when she was nervous, felt her underarms bathed with cold perspiration. At long last Scilla arrived, alone, threading her way through the tables towards my mother in her little fawn coat; the straw-coloured shock of hair was wind-blown and she peered around her short-sightedly with a vague, abstracted air. What a ridiculous little person she is, my mother thought suddenly, and that little coat of hers, too, how shabby and ridiculous it looks. Scilla's appearance seemed to have deteriorated since my mother had first met her, and today she looked weary and depressed. But why was she alone? Nothing she could do about it, said Scilla as she sat down, not a chance of Valeria's being able to do anything for the time being: Valeria's husband had had a fall from his horse and had broken three ribs; he had been taken to hospital and Valeria couldn't leave him. And that wasn't all: Valeria's lover might be going to leave her; so, what with one thing and another, poor Valeria was in no state to discuss loans at the moment; she was beside herself with worry; her husband refused to let her leave him alone for a second, he was like a spoilt child; and when Valeria wanted to have a good cry, she had to shut herself in the W.C. So what was to happen, asked my mother, so disappointed that she felt like having a good cry herself; and she felt suddenly very tired and her arms and legs were numb, because she had waited so long for this moment and now nothing was going to happen. So, said Scilla, they would just have to wait; what could she do; she was really depressed; and now, if you please, she had yet another problem with Barbara.

When she left for the country house, she had arranged for Barbara to stay with one of her school-friends, in the mother's charge, but naturally she had left her the flat keys in case she needed anything, like books or a pair of stockings, while she was away; then, when she returned and went to fetch Barbara from her friend's house they told her that she had gone out after dinner and they had no idea where she was. Hurrying to the flat in Via Tripoli, what should Scilla find but

Barbara and Pinuccio alone there together; and they'd been there alone, in the bedroom, for at least two hours. Scilla thought they both looked decidedly flustered. She had returned a day earlier than she had said, so they were certainly not expecting her to turn up; Barbara had red marks like thumb-prints on her neck and the bedcover was all rumpled. Scilla ordered Pinuccio to follow her into the sitting-room and told Barbara to go and wash her face, comb her hair and tidy herself up; then she closeted herself in the sitting-room with Pinuccio and told him flatly that if he did not marry Barbara immediately she would go to the police and file a complaint against him for trespass, corruption of a minor and breach of promise. Pinuccio insisted that he firmly intended to marry Barbara and was only waiting for his family's consent; never mind that, said Scilla, they would manage without their consent; besides, Pinuccio was over twenty-five, had his own place in Catania and sufficient income to support them.

My mother reproached Scilla for having left Barbara with-out adequate supervision; this would never have happened if Scilla had not gone gallivanting off to that wretched country house. Whyever had she not entrusted Barbara to her, instead of leaving her with a family she hardly knew? Why, indeed, had she not sent her to stay with Gilberto? Gilberto, Scilla explained, lived in one tiny room where there was barely space enough for his camp-bed; and he led an irregular sort of life, often staying out half the night playing cards with his friends. Perhaps my mother was right, and she should have left Barbara with her; Barbara loved being with us, particularly with Giulia; they had become very close friends, Barbara and Giulia, and Scilla was sure that Giulia's sweet, gentle nature would be a good influence; but she had been afraid that Barbara might be a nuisance to my mother. Quite the contrary, said my mother; still, things might have worked out for the best if Pinuccio was now going to marry Barbara without delay, and Scilla would have to start thinking about the trousseau. Hang the trousseau, said Scilla; there was no time now to mess about with a trousseau: Pinuccio was to sit his final law exams in a few days' time, and she had insisted that before the month was up, the two of them should be husband and wife.

So in a very little while, said Scilla, she would be even more on her own, and it was vital that she should have some occupation, or she would lose all interest in life; they must forge on with the shop, and if no loan was to be had from Valeria, well, she would sink all her own small capital into the business even if it meant that she would be destitute in her old age and have to beg on the church steps. My mother agreed: *Sagittarius* must not be abandoned; they could manage without Valeria; by pooling their savings they could start up a little shop tomorrow. Scilla produced a pencil, moistened the lead with her tongue and began to scribble calculations on the paper napkin provided with their cups of chocolate; because my mother, deciding that they needed some comfort, had ordered two cups of hot chocolate with whipped cream. My mother tried to follow Scilla's calculations but she was soon lost; her thoughts were reeling dizzily from Pinuccio and Barbara to Valeria and her lover, the husband and the hospital, Gilberto on his camp-bed and *Sagittarius*; Scilla had this extra-ordinary power of filling her head with images, and my mother could remember so well how, before she had met Scilla, her life had been drab and empty.

For a time Scilla was busy with all the preparations for the wedding. Having first dismissed the idea of a trousseau as out of the question, she had decided that a minimum, at least, had to be provided. Too agitated to sleep, she spent night after night embroidering linen with a delicate tracery of stitches. She was very skilled at embroidery, having been educated, as a small child, at a school run by nuns. Barbara no longer went to school now, but lazed around the flat watching and waiting for Pinuccio. Her mother had forbidden her to leave the house in case she might be tempted to flirt with the boys. Her one concession was visits to Giulia, and the two girls would often spend the entire afternoon together, sitting on the ottoman in the dining-room or standing at the window watching the trains go by; and Barbara put her arm around Giulia's waist, now thickened by her pregnancy, and said that she wanted six children, three boys and three girls; and she also wanted an Alsatian, a monkey and a cageful of parrots, all pets that she had longed for since she was a child. But she didn't want any cats at all, because Menelao, her Siamese, had had a fight on the roof-top and had lost an eye; he looked terrible and had probably been in pain, too, so they had telephoned the Animal Welfare people to come and collect him. So no more cats, because they would always remind her of her own poor little kitten. Pinuccio was being very good at the moment and had stopped being so jealous. He had written to his family and told them that he was getting married and they had not been as angry as he expected. His sisters had sent Barbara a home-made cake stuffed with raisins and walnuts and almonds and she had eaten nearly all of it in one go, and her face had come out in spots all over. Yes, she probably would end up in Sicily when she was married, but she was getting used to the idea now; and perhaps Pinuccio's sisters were nicer than she had thought.

So the wedding took place: a very low-key affair. Scilla came to tell my mother that the ceremony was to take place the following day in the church of Saint Peter and Saint Paul at five o'clock in the evening. My mother asked why they had decided on an evening wedding; only widows or pregnant girls were usually married in the evening; and why that particular church, the darkest in the town? Scilla said that the decision had been Pinuccio's; he was in a very bad mood again and didn't want any guests at the wedding except us, because he knew that we were such good friends; he had banned all other guests because some evil person had written to his father telling him all kinds of lies about Barbara, Scilla and Gilberto; and his father had believed it all and the day before, Pinuccio had had a letter from him packed with insults; and his mother, a poor, timid little woman who had always been her husband's slave and had worn herself out working in a dark kitchen, had secretly

112

written him a few tear-splashed lines enclosing a ruby ring. This was why Pinuccio was so down and had decided against any fuss. But he had kept all this from Barbara to avoid upsetting her and she was preparing for her wedding in the firm belief that everything had been sorted out with his family, and she was disappointed that there was to be no reception. After the wedding, Pinuccio and Barbara were leaving for Catania to set up house in a small apartment that Pinuccio owned, and attempt a reconciliation with his family.

I had to go to the wedding: my mother came round to fetch me, insisting that I change my old sweater for the blouse that she had bought me for the occasion so that I should not disgrace her. She herself was dressed to the nines in a black suit beneath her fur coat: she was secretly hoping for the chance to impress Valeria. But Valeria was not there; Scilla said that she had gone to Ischia for treatment in the mud baths. The only other people there, apart from my mother and myself, Giulia and Chaim, were Gilberto and his partridge-shooting friend, dressed in a raincoat and a Basque beret. Barbara looked wonderful: she wore a pale blue dress, short, straight and simple; and her flaming hair was gathered into a big chignon and covered by a little bridal veil. And as my mother followed the service, she was touched and she felt the old wound re-open as she watched Pinuccio, tall, young and physically sound in his dark-blue double-breasted suit, with languid eyes and long black hair curling softly at the nape of his neck and compared this with the bent, twitching figure of Chaim.

After the service we went to the coffee-bar, the same one my mother always went to. The waiter knew Scilla and my mother fairly well by this time, and he came to offer his congratulations. We all sat down around a table, Scilla ordered pastries and white wine and we toasted the bride and groom. Gilberto and his friend sat slightly apart from the rest, engrossed in some private conversation, Gilberto nodding solemnly and stroking his moustache and then suddenly bursting into a shrill cackle of laughter that sounded like gun-fire. Every time this happened, Pinuccio shuddered and his face darkened, and

113

he shot a sideways glance at the two men from dark, languid eyes, clenched his teeth and drummed his fingers on the table. Barbara sat beside him, stroking the lapels of his camel-hair coat with her plump, freckled hand and then replacing the hairpins in her chignon which was beginning to work loose and hang down on her neck, ready to transform itself back into a pony-tail. Scilla, in her hoarse, high-pitched voice, asked Chaim's advice about Gilberto's ulcer, an ulcer that he had had for years and neglected, because he would smoke and drink whisky and cognac and refused to listen to any advice about diets. Gilberto said that apart from the ulcer, he had a parasite in his gut, picked up in Albania when he was in the army; but his friend in the Basque beret shouted at him to give over all this talk about ulcers and all his other rotten ailments: this was supposed to be a wedding celebration.

After a few glasses of wine, Scilla became excited and tearful and buried her head in my mother's fur coat. But Gilberto said there was no time for tears, it was late already and they had a train to catch and still had to collect the suitcases from home. They called a taxi and my mother insisted on going with them to see them off; and Gilberto's friend in the Basque beret rode off on his Lambretta, waving a large leather glove.

Chaim, Giulia and I set off for home together; and Giulia wept silently with bowed head, chewing a finger of her glove; and Chaim said it was certainly sad that Barbara was going to live so far away in Sicily, because she had been a good friend for Giulia to have. But Barbara's mother, that Scilla woman, said Chaim, he did not like at all; and he couldn't stand the way she painted. And he liked Gilberto even less, and could not understand what pleasure my mother found in the company of such people. I told him that I too did not like them very much. But Giulia said nothing, and continued to suck her thumb through the glove and weep.

That evening, after the bridal couple had left, my mother went with Scilla and Gilberto to a small restaurant near Via

Tripoli and Scilla explained to Gilberto all about *Sagittarius*. Gilberto stroked his moustache as he listened, then made a non-committal gurgling noise in his throat and sat in silence for some time, stroking his moustache, rubbing his bald pate and looking sideways. Eventually, when he was on the point of leaving, he said that Crovetto, his friend with the Basque beret, had mentioned that there was a place for sale, a place in a good central position that used to be a haberdashery. Scilla asked him to ring Crovetto straight away, and with some reluctance he bought a token at the counter and went to make the call, putting a hand over his other ear to shut out the noise.

They were asking six million lire for the place. According to Crovetto, it was an absolute bargain: it was in the busiest part of town, on the corner between Via della Vigna and Via Monteverdi and right next to a well-known pastry-shop. Crovetto knew the owner personally and had agreed to take them to his office, an estate agency in Via San Cosimo, the next day; Gilberto, too, knew the man slightly. After Gilberto had left, my mother and Scilla stayed chatting for a long time, then went outside and walked up and down in the shelter of the tram terminus. My mother had invested a little over five million in her Italgas shares; Scilla's Incet shares should realize about three million. What they should do, said my mother, was to persuade the owner to let them have the place for an immediate down-payment of four million; they could then pay the rest by monthly instalments.

The next day, Scilla came to the house early to collect my mother. They were to meet Gilberto and Crovetto in the pastry-shop in Via della Vigna; they had a few pastries while they waited, but Crovetto soon arrived on his Lambretta with Gilberto crouched on the pillion. The shop was there on the corner, its windows covered with whitewash; inside, one could glimpse men with ladders repainting the walls.

They went to find the proprietor. He lived quite close, down a long, narrow passage-way through an arch where a photographer had his shop; filing through the shadowy passage-way past photographs of smiling girls and posing officers, they came to a door marked 'Pacini & Co.' that jangled a little bell as they opened it. A woman with peroxide-blonde hair emerged, manicuring her nails; she introduced herself as the owner's wife and led them into a small sitting-room, opening the shutters to reveal yellow satin drapes. As they sat down, she went on buffing her nails with a piece of chamois leather; she, Gilberto and Crovetto appeared to be on familiar terms and started to chat about a friend called Gaspare who had won some poker game. In answer to a question about the shop, she said yes, as far as she knew it was up for sale but she had no idea of the price; her husband was away in Genoa at the moment and would be back in about ten days. They went on chatting, Gilberto, Crovetto and the blonde, recalling an evening when they had teased a girl called Maria; Maria, it seemed, had eventually fled in tears. Gilberto gave his shrill cackle of laughter at the memory, but my mother felt that her sympathies were entirely on the side of the girl. My mother was feeling very uneasy in that room all done out in yellow and with an enormous shell hanging on the wall and a bunch of waving ostrich feathers in a vase; ostrich feathers are unlucky.

So it was a relief when Scilla stood up briskly, buttoned up her coat, shook her straw-coloured shock of hair and declared that they would come back in ten days' time. The blonde invited Gilberto and Crovetto to stay for a while; they could ask Gaspare, who lived on the floor above, to come down for a game of poker, and she would cook them all a mushroom soufflé for lunch. She dismissed Scilla coldly, neither looking at her nor shaking her hand, and thrust a limp paw vaguely towards my mother. As the door jangled to behind them, my mother fancied she heard Gilberto's cackle, shrill and staccato like gunfire; she felt even more uneasy and very tired, and she longed to be home; and she felt a sense of shame, as if she had been ridiculed. But Scilla took her arm and said she was furious: Crovetto had had the effrontery to take them to the house of his mistress, a woman of doubtful reputation, a shameless hussy. How dreadful of Crovetto to have shown such disrespect to my mother; what cheek to take her to a

116

place such as that; she had nearly told him what she thought of him, right there in front of his fancy-woman. Eventually it was my mother who had to comfort Scilla, reminding her that it was necessary, after all, that they deal with the owner. But Scilla said that from now on Gilberto and Crovetto would act on their behalf, because they would never stoop to enter such a place again. My mother asked Scilla if she knew what had happened to the girl, Maria, who had been teased until she cried; but Scilla said she had no idea who she was. Just look at the kind of people Gilberto goes round with nowadays, she said, and fancy him spending his days drinking whisky and playing poker. He was becoming cold and cynical, too, if he found it amusing to make a girl cry. Scilla and my mother went to have another look at the shop; it was midday now, the workmen had disappeared for lunch and the shutters were down; so they stood outside for a while watching to see if the right sort of smart people passed by. Finally, before going home, they returned to the pastry-shop, because the mention of mushroom soufflé had made my mother hungry.

Scilla then left for Valeria's country estate, and stayed away for more than a week. Valeria had returned from Ischia and was trying to forget her lover, who had now definitely left her; she wanted Scilla to keep her company while she destroyed all the letters and mementos of that unworthy man and went on long walks through the huge fields where the horses grazed. And her husband, who was now convalescent, had been told to rest; and he also wanted Scilla there to keep him company and talk to him about her time as secretary to the deputy; Valeria's husband was always curious to know all about deputies because he had political ambitions himself, and although he was so tight-fisted, he had spent out vast sums to further this ambition, and had financed a left-wing paper since becoming disillusioned with the right.

While Scilla was away, my mother spent most of her time at home keeping Giulia company. The days were warmer now and they sat out in the sun side by side, my mother working on a little jacket for the baby using a stitch Scilla had taught her, a variety of cross-stitch; strange, how Scilla seemed to be obsessed with crosses: nearly everything she did seemed to have crosses in it in one form or another. As she was sitting with Giulia, my mother was tempted to tell her about *Sagittarius*. Maybe Giulia would even welcome the idea of working in the shop, it would do her good to have something to occupy her; but at the last moment she resisted the temptation; she rearranged the rug over Giulia's knees, picked one or two hairs from her dress and slapped the puppy who was chewing playfully at Giulia's white, blue-veined arms.

One day my mother found a letter from Barbara in a pocket of Giulia's jacket; it only consisted of a few untidy lines full of blots and crossings-out. Barbara wrote from Catania and said that things were not going well, but did not explain why; she was very homesick for the flat in Via Tripoli, her mother, Giulia and even the classroom which she used to think so boring; she ended by saying that her youth was now a thing of the past. Having read the hastily-scribbled letter full of spelling mistakes and schoolgirl sentimentality, my mother put it back in the envelope and replaced it in Giulia's pocket; then she put on her beret and hurried to Via Tripoli. She knew that Scilla should be back by now and she wanted to warn her as soon as possible that something was seriously wrong in Catania.

Reading the letter had given my mother a covert sense of pleasure; when things were going badly for someone else, she always felt a little thrill of pleasure disguised beneath an urgent desire for action; and on her way to Via Tripoli she rehearsed what she would say to Scilla, reproving her for marrying off her daughter far too young.

Standing at Scilla's door, she pressed the doorbell hard; and after a while, after much scraping of chairs and clicking of locks, Scilla appeared in the doorway; she was wearing a dressing-gown and looked very sleepy; she was tying the girdle and pulling the lapels of the faded, shabby little robe across her chest. She told my mother to come in, and my mother found that the flat was all in darkness and the shutters were still closed. Scilla explained that she had only been back for a few hours; she seemed less than happy to see my mother and kept rubbing her eyes as if she had not slept for a week; she listened to my mother's story about Barbara's letter but seemed unworried by it: the first months of a marriage were bound to be difficult, but Barbara had patience and common sense and Pinuccio was a nice boy; they had probably had a little argument so Barbara had written a weepy letter; but her own letters from Barbara told quite another story; and Barbara had sent her postcards from Naples, Pompeii and from Capri where she had bought herself a pair of fisherman's trousers. My mother remarked that Barbara's behind was rather too big for trousers to look good on her; and Scilla was offended and said that Barbara's behind was not at all too big, but that her measurements were exactly the same as Ava Gardner's. Then Scilla asked my mother to go: she had to give the flat a good cleaning and wanted to wash the windows, polish the floor and air the mattresses. My mother rose to leave, feeling thoroughly offended in her turn, and asked Scilla why she had still not engaged that manservant she was talking so much about, the one who was related to Valeria's chauffeur.

My mother was in a black mood as she came away from Scilla's flat. It was three o'clock in the afternoon and beginning to get hot, she had no idea what to do with herself and the day stretched emptily before her. She had the impression that Scilla had been in a great hurry to see the back of her and that she had been almost bodily pushed out of the door. She had the feeling, too, that there had been someone else in the flat apart from herself and Scilla, though she could not have explained why she had this feeling.

After wandering aimlessly for a while, she went into a cinema. They were showing a film in colour about African safaris, and she sat in the half-empty auditorium watching endless herds of buffalo seen against a boundless, fiery-red horizon; there was no plot, nothing actually happened and one saw nothing except buffalo, bison and elephants. With no plot to engage her interest, she was soon bored; and her thoughts kept returning to the darkened flat and to Scilla wandering around tying up her dressing-gown girdle; and there was no doubt that she *had* pushed her out of the door, and locked it behind her with a vicious snap. And she had hardly listened to what she had been saying about Barbara's letter, almost as if she wanted to wash her hands of the whole business of her daughter and not worry any more about her. On her way out of the cinema my mother passed a poster advertising next week's programme, a film with Ava Gardner, and she looked at Ava Gardner's behind that had the same measurements as Barbara's and sniffed scornfully.

She then came up to my flat; I was in the middle of a lesson, so she waited, sitting in an armchair and reading the afternoon paper. Every now and then she commented aloud on the political articles; and she kept asking my pupil, a college student with an alarmingly white face and an air of constant perplexity, if she did not agree with her. When the girl had gone, my mother suggested that we go together to the coffee-bar; but I had too much studying to do and refused. She was very put out, and asked me where I thought all this studying would get me: when I graduated I would end up teaching in some drab school facing a whole pack of girls with white, pasty faces and puzzled expressions like this one who had just left. It had not been a good idea at all for me to study literature, she said as she put on her gloves; I should have studied chemistry or law instead. As a child, I had seemed to have a real gift for writing, but I had written nothing at all since then. Or I could have studied medicine: many women nowadays became doctors, and were even more sought-after than the men because so many women refused to be examined by men; and all doctors, besides, made a lot of money — apart from Chaim, of course, who was a disaster. But I was feeling cross too, and to annoy her I asked why she had not set Chaim up in his own practice yet; she retorted that she had not the slightest intention of doing so and, on the contrary, was planning something quite different. And she swept out, slamming the door behind her. But seconds later she came back again, on the pretext that she had left her scarf behind; it was on the chair, and as I handed it to her I said, to pacify her, how pretty it was; and she immediately made me a present of it, saying that she had plenty of scarves, enough and to spare for the parish poor, and she put it round my neck. She embraced me and asked me to forgive her for being cross and said I was her only comfort: she could at least hold a conversation with me, whereas Giulia never opened her mouth; Giulia was capable of going for days without uttering a word, and made no effort even to be pleasant to her husband; she never looked at him or spoke to him and moved away if he so much as touched her knee. Theirs was not a happy marriage. How often, said my mother, it would be better for a woman to stay single rather than marry the wrong man; and she told me to think well before I married and talk it over thoroughly with her, something Giulia had never done. Did I have a boyfriend? I shook my head furiously and turned away with a frown; and she changed the subject at once, fearing to annoy me again. Perhaps, she said, the solution for a woman was to have an occupation. She enquired after my friend, who was now married and on her honeymoon; she wanted to know if my friend was happy with that engineer with the ears; and she wanted to know if I was still determined to stay on alone in the little flat.

I had put some water on to boil in the kitchen with a stock cube dissolved in it to make some soup; was this all the supper I would have, my mother asked; no egg, no meat? I assured her that I also had some stewed fruit and cheese, but she was not satisfied, she thought this insufficient, that I was stinting myself and said that food was the one thing one should never try to economize on. I assured her that I had all I needed, but she insisted on giving me ten thousand lire so that I could get some little luxury. Then she scrutinized my clothes. I had at last stopped wearing the Russian workman's sweater and had on a check dress: not too bad, said my mother, though it reminded her of an orphanage. She told me about the film she had just seen, with the bison and buffalo; rather dreary, but the views were beautiful; and she said that maybe sometime in the future, if a certain project was successful, the two of us would be able to travel a bit, maybe even venturing as far as Africa on a summer cruise. If, she said with a little smirk, a certain project turned out successfully. She would love to go abroad. For this cruise, she said, we would get the dressmaker to make us each a white suit. A little man she knew had offered her, at five hundred lire the metre, an absolute bargain, a certain white stuff with a slightly rough finish like fine towelling. She left then, and as I watched her from the window, crossing the square with her confident step and her handbag swinging at her hip, I knew that she was imagining herself lounging on the deck of a cruise-liner in sunglasses and a suit made from a stuff with a slightly rough finish, leafing through magazines and talking to the captain.

That evening Scilla phoned my mother to tell her that the owner of the shop had agreed to sell, but he insisted on their paying five million straight away; the rest could be paid off in monthly instalments of seventy thousand. Scilla sounded in the best of spirits, and she seemed to have forgotten all about her very cold reception of my mother that very afternoon; and my mother promptly forgot about it too. As Giulia and Costanza were in the same room with her, she could only reply to Scilla in monosyllables, but she arranged to meet her the following day.

They met in their usual coffee-bar. For once, Scilla was there first; and she was very annoyed at being kept waiting. She seemed to be in a bad temper again, she had bags under her eyes and her coarse, putty-like skin was drawn and lined. She said she was unwell and that she had eaten too much, as usual, while staying with Valeria. She swallowed a pill with a glass of mineral water then told my mother to order quickly, but not granita with whipped cream: the very smell would put her off. But cream, observed my mother, had no smell.

Scilla said that they must get hold of five million immediately, there was not a moment to be lost because the vendor needed the money at once and somebody else had already made him an offer. My mother would put up the five million and she, Scilla, would pay back her half as soon as she had sold her Incet shares; she could not sell them that day because they were being quoted very low and she would stand to lose on the transaction; Italgas, on the other hand, were doing well. She showed my mother the share prices in a newspaper, and my mother looked at the column of figures and nodded silently though the figures meant nothing to her, inexpert as she was.

Then my mother phoned her stockbroker and asked him to make the capital available to her that very morning; and she phoned home to say that she would be out for lunch because she was going to eat with Scilla, and would be back in the evening.

She went alone into the stockbroker's office, leaving Scilla, who was feeling cold, sitting on a bench outside in the sun. My mother was in the office for some time; the place was crowded and she was asked to wait in a lobby; and she was so excited and nervous that she smoked one cigarette after another. At last, with the five million in a yellow envelope at the bottom of her old, stout leather handbag, and the bag clutched tightly under a damp armpit, she emerged and rejoined Scilla.

Now, said Scilla, they would go to her place, have a spot of lunch and relax for a while, and phone Gilberto and Crovetto to let the vendor know that the money was available; then they would go with the vendor to the solicitor to sign the contract.

They called a taxi to take them to Via Tripoli; and in the taxi, my mother opened her bag just a crack and peeped at the yellow envelope held by an elastic band nestling beside her comb and red lacquer powder-compact. My mother felt a sudden urge to giggle, but Scilla sat huddled bad-temperedly in a corner of the seat with her coat-collar turned up to her chin, constantly complaining of feeling cold; she was shivery, possibly feverish, and said she would take her temperature as soon as she got home. My mother paid for the taxi at her own

123

insistence because, she said, with all that money on her, she felt rich, as rich as a Rothschild; and Scilla had no objection, but went to make a phone-call from the bakery.

They went up to the flat and waited, sitting on the balcony, for Gilberto to arrive. Scilla put the envelope with the money in a drawer of the dressing-table and gave the key to my mother because, she said, she was so scatterbrained herself that she might lose it. For lunch, Scilla fried a cutlet for my mother but she herself only had a little boiled chicory and a cup of black coffee. The cutlet was tasty but slightly overdone whereas my mother liked her meat rare; but Scilla had been ironing a petticoat while it was cooking and had been distracted. They ate in the kitchen, pushing the ironing cloth to one side and using the bare table; and Scilla produced a bottle of Barolo, a present from Crovetto, and poured out a large glass for my mother; she drank none herself because Barolo was a wine she hadn't touched in years.

They lit cigarettes and went out onto the balcony to smoke. My mother suddenly remembered that Scilla had wanted to take her temperature; but Scilla said she felt quite well now. She still looked pale, however, and very tense, and kept rolling up her belt and undoing and doing up the buttons of her gabardine dress, a pale yellow dress exactly the same colour as her hair. My mother confessed that she too was feeling tense; and no wonder, considering the big step they were about to take; but as soon as they had the contract in their hands they would feel much better. They leant against the railings in the warm sunshine, and my mother said that when they were old maybe they could retire together to some little village on the Riviera, one of those places where old ladies went to live cheaply and enjoy the sea air. Scilla said that sounded really nice, and that perhaps when she was old she would be able to enjoy a bit of peace and quiet at last, and it was no more than she deserved after all she had been through, more trials and tribulations than my mother could possibly imagine; she had never had any luck: it had been her fate to be kicked around all her life. As they waited, the afternoon wore on, the sun disappeared from the balcony and eventually Scilla complained of feeling cold again; and my mother, from gazing down for so long at the street so far below their aerial perch on the balcony, began to feel giddy. Scilla suggested she go and lie down for a little, so my mother took off her shoes and lay down on Scilla's bed under a coverlet of periwinkle blue and with a photograph of Barbara aged seven, dressed in white for her first communion, on the bedside table.

My mother's eyelids felt heavy and her head seemed to be encased in a band of iron; it occurred to her that perhaps the wine had disagreed with her. She saw Scilla sitting at the foot of the bed, and she seemed to be dwindling, dwindling and getting further and further away until the putty-coloured skin and the shock of yellow hair dissolved into thin air; then she noticed Scilla closing the shutters and pulling the blue coverlet up to her chin, and she wanted to thank her but only just managed to caress her dress with a hand that she could hardly lift; and then she felt herself falling, falling, falling, sinking to the bottom of a dark lake where nothing mattered any more.

When she awoke, it took my mother a few moments to remember where she was. The sight of the periwinkle-blue coverlet began to bring things gradually back to her. She got up and groped in the dark for her shoes on the bedside mat; then she called out to Scilla, doing up her dress and rearranging her hair. She still felt the band around her head and her legs were still heavy, so she called out to Scilla that the wine had certainly disagreed with her, there must have been something wrong with it.

There was no reply. Still calling, she went out into the passage; it occurred to her that Scilla might have gone downstairs to make a phone-call. The shutters were closed in the bedroom and sitting room, but those in the kitchen were open, and my mother saw that it was now dark outside. She looked at her watch: it said ten o'clock. Goodness, how ever long had she slept? Nearly eight hours! Scilla must have gone to phone them at home, to tell them that she would not be back for a while, she thought; and the appointment with the solicitor had probably been put off until tomorrow and that was why they had let her sleep undisturbed for so long.

She turned on the light in the living room: there was paper and string all over the floor and chaos everywhere. Returning to the bedroom, she noticed that the wardrobe where Scilla kept her clothes was half-open and now empty, and Barbara's photograph had gone; indeed, all the photographs and pictures had gone from the walls. Driven by a rising tide of panic, she rummaged through her handbag in search of the key that Scilla had given her for safe-keeping; then she emptied her bag onto the bedcover, and out came a shower of comb, handkerchief, powder-compact and address-book; but no key. She ran to the dressing-table; it stood in a corner of the room, a cactus in a small pot standing on it. Cactus plants were unlucky.

And there it was, the little key, inserted into the lock of the top drawer. My mother wrenched open all the drawers: every one was empty; the top drawer, where Scilla had put the envelope, was empty, and the next, and the next; they were all empty. All she found, stuffed right at the back of the top drawer, were a pair of silk stockings rolled into a ball and a torn pink vest.

Now she understood everything. Raising her head, my mother saw her face in the mirror, deeply creased, swollen and covered with red blotches. She went all round the flat: all the cutlery had gone from the kitchen dresser and only the plates were left; the small room where Scilla had kept her paintings was empty; in the bathroom, the shabby little dressing-gown was hanging on a hook; in the kitchen, a bowl containing a spike of cooked chicory like a green bullet still stood on the table, and there was a stalk of celery in a glass.

She had been tricked: she had been duped and swindled just like the wretched people one read about in the papers. Scilla had planned everything; she had brought her back to the flat and put a sleeping-draught in the wine; and while she slept her drugged sleep, she had got away with her money. She had taken from the flat everything that she owned, leaving only the furniture, which was the property of the landlord. And for my mother she had left nothing at all, nothing apart from an old pair of stockings and a bullet of chicory.

My mother sat down at the table in the kitchen and began to sob; and as she sobbed she clashed her necklace against her chest and pressed the palm of a shaking hand to her lips; and the sobs tore themselves out of her from the depths of her heart bringing with them a surge of self-pity in which there was no sweetness at all, a self-pity that was utterly desolate and as black as night. My mother never wanted to see Giulia, or Chaim or me ever again, and she never wanted to do anything ever again.

But quite suddenly she was overwhelmed by such a sense of disgust with the empty flat, the kitchen and the chicory, that she seized her beret and her handbag and fled down the stairs. The door to the courtyard could be opened from the inside; my mother went through it, crossed the courtyard and knocked on the mattress-maker's door, where she could see a sliver of light. There was no official porter here, and the mattress-maker did duty as a concierge. While she waited for the woman to open the door, my mother smeared away the tears with her fingers and pushed her hair back from her face; and then the mattress-maker came, looking surprised and slightly annoyed because she had been about to go to bed. My mother asked whether Signora Fontana had left any message for her when she left. No, said the woman, no message; she had told her that my mother was in the flat and might be staying there for a day or two, had called a taxi as she had three heavy suitcases with her, and, saying that she would be back soon, had left without giving her a forwarding address but asking the mattress-maker to collect and keep all her mail for her, and had left a whole bunch of keys belonging to the flat with her just in case anything should happen.

Sobbing, my mother made her way home. She walked the whole way, because if she took the tram, people would see her crying, and she would not even take a taxi because she now felt as poor as a church mouse; and besides, she had only a few coins in her purse. So she walked right through the town; and every now and then she leant against a wall, sobbing, but if anyone stopped to look at her, she started walking again; and she clutched her bag with those few coins in it very tightly because she had the feeling that everybody was out to rob her. She had no house-keys on her, so she rang the door-bell.

After a while, Carmela came to open the door; she was half asleep and had on her mackintosh over her nightdress. Chaim and Giulia, she said, had gone to bed some time ago; they had not been expecting her to return at all that evening, because Signora Fontana had rung during the afternoon to say that she and my mother were going off somewhere together and wouldn't be back until the next day. My mother told her to wake Chaim.

As soon as she got to her own room, my mother threw herself on her bed and began to scream; immediately the entire household gathered around her: Chaim, Giulia, Costanza, Carmela. My mother wept and screamed all night; and she wanted to tell them all that had happened, but was stammering and trembling so much that no one could understand her. Chaim gave her a sedative injection and, cradling her head in his arms, forced her, against her will, to drink some bitter liquid.

Very early the next morning Chaim and my mother went to the police; because Chaim had succeeded in piecing together some of the story from my mother's broken sentences. My mother learned from the police that Scilla's real name was Antonietta Grossi and that she and Gilberto had already been implicated in a fraud involving forged promissory notes some years ago. The inspector, who showed little patience with my mother, told her that there was not the slightest chance of recovering her money; she was welcome to file a complaint, but she apparently had no proof that she had handed over the money; and he told her that despite all her grey hairs, she had acted with the circumspection of a four-year-old.

Enquiries revealed that Signora Antonietta Grossi, together

with her husband and a third individual wearing a black Basque beret, had taken the train for Ventimiglia; they were over the border and to try to trace them would be like looking for a needle in a haystack. A police officer accompanied my mother and Chaim to the office of Pacini & Co. where the same blonde woman as before answered the door and led them into the same little room. She very vaguely remembered having seen my mother before, but with so many people coming and going in the office it was difficult to be certain. Her husband had been away from town for more than three months; she and her husband knew Gilberto, but only vaguely, and his friend Crovetto to whom, incidentally, they had lent some money; they had no shop for sale on the corner of Via Monteverdi as far as she knew, but then she knew nothing about her husband's business. My mother then became hysterical and Chaim had to call a taxi and take her home.

It transpired that the real owner of the shop was a wholesale merchant who, far from intending to sell the place, was thinking of setting up an ale-shop there. And it also transpired that Signora Antonietta Grossi, alias Priscilla Fontana, owed her landlord several months' rent for the flat in Via Tripoli and had also left considerable sums owing to the baker, the dairy-man and the butcher; and my mother brooded on the fact that not even the cutlet that Scilla had cooked for her that day, not even that one cutlet, had Scilla paid for out of her own pocket. And the landlord, after speaking to the mattress-maker, came to my mother whining about hardship and begging her to pay her friend's rent arrears, because the mattress-maker had told him that Scilla and my mother were such close friends and might even be distantly related.

I went to stay with my mother for a time. But she seemed not to want my company, nor even that of Giulia. She stayed in her room, crying and smoking and writing one letter after another in her tall, narrow handwriting in which the stroke over the T took up a whole line. She wrote to Barbara, to Pinuccio and, having got their address from Giulia, to Pinuccio's parents; and she wrote to cousin Teresa's husband, the solicitor begging him, however, not to tell any other member of the family. The only reply she received was from the solicitor; from the others, nothing. She never went back to her sisters' shop: the very thought of all those china knick-knacks made her feel ill, and she had no desire to see her sisters, who nevertheless came to see her several times to commiserate and shake their heads sympathetically. Her attitude towards the police was one of total mistrust now, even of unreasoning hatred, and nothing on earth would ever induce her to set foot in a police station again. Of all the people Scilla had talked about, my mother knew nothing apart from their forenames; the only surname she had mentioned was Valeria's: Lubrani. If Valeria was anything more than a figment of Scilla's imagination, she might be a Lubrani. There were six or seven entries in the telephone directory under this name, but my mother remembered that Scilla had once said that Valeria lived somewhere near the church of San Matteo. The phone book showed one Lubrani in Via Roma, not far from the church of San Matteo, and my mother immediately decided to go to the address shown. So for the first time in many days she dressed with care, even pinning the paste brooch, after much deliberation, to the lapel of her black suit.

She found a pleasant house with a neatly gravelled garden and a pool with a fountain. The door was opened by a manservant in a white jacket, and my mother asked him if she could see Signora Lubrani, adding that she did not know the lady personally but wished to ask her something. The man asked her to wait in the hall and my mother spent a few moments contemplating a Japanese painting of birds and almond-blossom; then she was shown into a study lined with bookshelves. There on a leather chair, dressed in black and with a fox-fur draped over one shoulder, sat a lady with a lantern-jaw, working deftly at a piece of crochet. This was Valeria.

Valeria waved my mother towards another leather armchair, and my mother sat down loosening the scarf around her throat to reveal the paste brooch. Then, in a low voice, trembling and uncertain, she asked if the signora was by any chance acquainted with a certain Priscilla Fontana. Valeria frowned for a moment in an effort to remember, then she brightened: Scilla Fontana, she exclaimed, the little dressmaker in Via Tripoli? Yes, indeed, she made those pretty blouses with a very delicate embroidery, but lately her sight had begun to fail and the collar of the last blouse she had made for her had been slightly crooked so she had not gone back to her. But she had not quite understood what my mother wanted: if it was the name of a dressmaker, she would gladly recommend a much better one.

My mother clasped her hands and began to tell her story. In telling her story, she had already braved the dismay of Giulia and Chaim and the sneer of the police inspector, now she rehearsed it once more to Valeria of the lantern jaw. She had suffered so much that she had to talk about it; and, indeed, she could no longer talk about anything else.

Valeria listened, alternately stroking her long chin and caressing the tail of her fox fur. When she finished, Valeria burst out laughing; her laughter was merry and unashamed and not unsympathetic, but she suppressed it at once with a jerk of her chin like a crane swallowing a fish.

She leant towards my mother and patted her knee with a broad, bony hand with big knuckles; and my mother caught a whiff of her perfume, the perfume that Scilla had called *coeur de lilas*. No, said Valeria, she had no country estate, anywhere; she did have a tiny holiday-house at Pallanza, but she had never taken Scilla there and doubted whether she had ever mentioned it to her. On the few occasions when they had met, the only thing she had ever discussed with Scilla was blouses, blouses, blouses, nothing but blouses. And as for her husband, he was the director of an historical archive; he had no political ambitions and had not been on a horse for the last twenty years.

Valeria accompanied my mother to the front door. Spreading her hands in a gesture of helplessness, she said how sorry she was to be unable to help, but she knew absolutely nothing more about Scilla Fontana. Unfortunately, the world was full of people who delighted in deceiving their fellows; and now that she came to think about it, she had always thought that there was something a bit strange about Scilla, even slightly suspicious; and once, when she had been to Scilla's flat for a fitting, she had left her umbrella behind, the kind that folds up to fit in a handbag, or at least she had been practically sure that that was where she left it, but Scilla said she had not seen it so she thought she must have left it somewhere else; now, however, she was convinced that Scilla had kept it. Fancy stealing an umbrella! Perhaps she was slightly mad.

After this visit to Valeria many days passed before my mother ventured out of the house again. She had stopped writing letters, she had even stopped crying. There were times when Valeria's merry, unashamed laughter still rang in her ears; the laughter was humiliating but also salutary, because she was now determined that no one would ever laugh at her again. She sat in an armchair by the window, lost in thought, and watched the trains until they disappeared with a hiss, and she now worked with a crochet-hook as she had seen Valeria do, and crocheted a cot-cover for Giulia's baby just to keep her hands occupied.

At times she caught herself dreaming, deep down inside, of a long friendship with Valeria, of their working on some project together in that study lined with bookshelves; but she repressed such thoughts, dismissing them as woolly and un-realistic, productive of neither pleasure nor reward. And she reminded herself that she was old and that her life was over.

Eventually she began to go out again; but every corner, every inch of the road, brought back some memory of Scilla. Here was the coffee-bar where they always went together, there the church where Barbara had been married, the hair-dresser's where they had first met, the cinema where they had seen a film together. Everywhere the little fawn coat had flitted, the yellow shock of hair blown in the wind; it seemed an age to my mother since the yellow bob had fluttered beside her shoulder, as distant in time as the years of happiness seem to one who has fallen on evil times, as the games of childhood seem when we are on the point of dying. It had been a happy time, but now she had to cancel it from her memory: it had brought nothing but dust and ashes, and dust and ashes leave no regrets behind.

Jozek came one morning, bringing with him a newspaper bearing big photographs of Barbara and Pinuccio. The paper reported that, at the Hotel Passaggero in Catania, one Pinuccio Scardillo had shot his young bride Barbara Scardillo née Grossi, aged nineteen, formerly of our town; the motive was apparently jealousy, the shooting having been preceded by a violent quarrel which had drawn all the other guests in the hotel to the scene; one of the hotel guests had rushed up and tried to wrest the gun away, but it was too late: Scardillo had fired. Barbara had been hit in the lung. She was dead.

Giulia immediately began to scream. She screamed and screamed, and Carmela, who was at the bottom of the garden, came running in thinking that Giulia was about to give birth. It was dreadful to see Giulia screaming like that: she pressed herself against the wall, clasping her temples and gazing ahead of her with eyes that were probably fixed upon a flaming red pony-tail.

Chaim had already left for the hospital, so I rang and went on ringing until I was able to speak to him and tell him to come home immediately. But by the time Chaim arrived, Giulia had already become much calmer: she lay on her bed with a rug over her legs, moaning softly; and my mother was holding her hand and applying wet towels to her forehead, not knowing what else she could do, apart from telling Jozek to get the hell out of her house with his wretched newspapers.

A few days later, my mother was sitting in the coffee-bar sipping a cold drink; she never ordered a granita now, the very mention of it was enough to make her shudder. And she thought she saw, in the distance, a shock of yellow hair above a little black dress; and she thought she recognized Scilla, in mourning, peering about her short-sightedly and dragging her feet slowly along the dusty road. My mother's first reaction was to leap up and run after her; but immediately a great weariness came over her, and she stayed where she was. The black figure was soon swallowed up in the crowd and my mother never knew whether it had been Scilla or merely some woman who resembled her. Anyway, it no longer mattered; but in the depths of her heart, where black hatred still seethed unquenched, she was surprised to discover a stirring of pity for the poor yellow bob.

In the summer, while giving birth to her child, my sister Giulia died. It was summer, a beautiful morning of high summer. Laid out on her bed, dressed in her bridal gown with her thin, blue-veined arms crossed over her breast and her lips parted slightly in a vague, sweet, melancholy smile, Giulia looked as though she were bidding farewell to this life, a life that she had never managed to love. In the next room, Giulia's baby, red in the face and with long, blond, Polish hair, cried in the arms of cousin Teresa who had arrived by coach the day before. Cousin Teresa sat in an armchair, rocking herself to and fro and cradling the baby, while my mother, suddenly very old and careworn, gazed at this unknown infant with dull, misty eyes. Silently, my mother looked at me, at Chaim, at cousin Teresa, at the unknown baby, imploring us with eyes in which the old brilliance was now drowned in a veil of tears, to give her back her Giulia. But the Giulia she wanted back was the little girl in the sailor-suit and black stockings, on whose lips no sad, timid smile had yet appeared. My mother understood that smile now. It was the smile of someone who wants nothing more than to be left alone to retreat softly into the shadows.